Romantic Rescue

Blake Allwood

Blake Allwood Publishing

Blake Allwood
Visit my website at www.blakeallwood.com

Printed in the United States of America
Box Elder, SD

Ebook ISBN: 978-1-956727-22-7
Paperback ISBN: 978-1-956727-20-3
Library of Congress Control Number: 2021922324

First Printing: September 2021

Content Warnings

Injury
Attempted Murder
Blood
Stalking
Car Accident
Head Injury
Violence
Death or Dying
Kidnapping and Abduction
Murder
False Allegations

Join Blake's email list to get advance notice of new books and receive his occasional newsletter:

www.blakeallwood.com

MM Romance **By Blake Allwood**	**Romantic Fantasy** **By Adam J. Ridley**

MM Romance
By Blake Allwood

Transitions Series
Aiden Inspired
Suzie Empowered (MF Romance)
Bobby Transformed

Chance Series
Love By Chance
Another Chance <u>With</u> Love
Taking A Chance <u>For</u> Love

Romantic Series
Romantic Renovations (1)
Romantic Rescue (2)
Romantic Recon (3)

Melody Series
Melody of the Heart
Melody of the Snow

Road to Rocktoberfest Anthology
Changing His Tune - 2022

Coming Home Series (2023)
A Long Way Home
Family Home
Discovering Home
Finding Home
Bound For Home
…and many more

Novellas
Tenacious
Moon's Place

Romantic Fantasy
By Adam J. Ridley

Big Bend Series
Love's Legacy (1)
Love's Heirloom (2)
Love's Bequest (3)

The Witch Brothers Series
Emerald Earth (1)
Diamond Air (2)
Ruby Fire (3)
Sapphire Water (4)

Acknowledgments

A special thank you to

John Gilchrist – Beta Reader
Ryan Eagan – Developmental Editor
Jo Bird - Copy Editor
Ann Attwood – Line Editor
Renee Mizar – Proofreader

A special thank you goes to all my friends and family who supported me, I couldn't have done it without you.
And of course, a big thank you to my husband who encourages me to keep going down these rabbit holes never knowing where I might end up.

One

P AIN RICOCHETED THROUGH ME, causing me to grind my teeth so hard that my jaw locked. Laying back, I squeezed my eyes shut and counted to twenty. "Damn it!" I yelled out when that didn't help.

Maybe it was the exertion, maybe it was the elevation, but the last thing I remembered was leaning on a tree for support when a swimming sensation overtook me. I woke up halfway down a landslide with one arm pinned under me and the mother of all headaches.

How long had I been down here? With an effort, I rolled off my arm and the throbbing instantly shifted from numbness to so intense I doubled over and gagged.

I must've passed out from it, because the next thing I remember was looking straight up into the sky as pain continued to pulse throughout my entire body. And now here I was, in agony and miles from anywhere.

I decided to stay still, hoping to minimize the pain. I just needed to get someone's attention. "Help!" I yelled. Each yell caused my arm to hurt even more! Despite that, I screamed until my ears rang and I could still hear my own voice echoing in my head.

Clearly, no one was coming – there was no one within miles of here *to* come! Slow and deliberately, I managed to lift my head up and look around. The sun was definitely lower than it had been when I fell. I reached for my phone trapped in the pocket under my injured arm, and was close to tears by the time I pulled it free.

Fighting the urge to vomit, I managed to look at the screen. It was five-thirty already, which meant at least two hours had passed. I thumbed nine-one-one and hit call, but there was no service. *Well, great! This just gets better by the moment.*

I tried, aww man did I try, but failed miserably in my efforts to sit up. And I although I'd never admit it to anyone, for a second there I wanted to cry like a baby. As my muscles seized and bunched in protest, I lay back in the mud and watched the water as it dripped from the trees after an earlier rain.

Eventually I gathered my strength and managed to get up, although it was easier said than done. The first challenge was standing up without passing out. Second was to maneuver up the rocky slide back to the trail. Earlier in the day, I'd averaged passing someone every twenty or thirty minutes. I was kind of annoyed that they were disturbing my peace. Now, I wanted nothing more than to see another human. I couldn't help but wonder where the hell they'd all disappeared to? My guess was that they were all smart enough not to get caught out on the trail in the evenings.

Every move I made brought agony and added another layer of despair, but I'd be damned before I let myself pass out again. In my mind I could hear my Tennessee folks chuckling.

"You'd think the boy was made out of glass or something."

Well, fuck them all. I might not be the manliest of my people, but I ain't no delicate flower either. If it was the last thing I did, I would *not* get stuck on this mountain all night. With my luck, a hungry bear would find my fairy-ass as tasty as salmon in the fall run.

Despite the pain, despite the effort to climb back up the mountain to the trail, my stupid ass mind decided to dredge up the shit that led me here in the first place.

"You're fired, you worthless heap, now get out!" The words of my *former* boss, stupid James McAllister, reverberated in my mind as I held my arm close.

Just six months earlier, that asshole had been under investigation for being involved in some shitstorm in Seattle. I'd defended him when the police came in asking questions, but the minute I do something out of line... Even though it was fucking justified, I mean I had every right to hit my unfriend Nathan in the nose after catching him kissing my boyfriend, right? But oh no... *I'm* the fucking worthless one. I'm the one that got fired. I'm the one who got kicked out... I'm the fucking one who had the cops called on him!

"Ugh," I moaned as I labored up the last of the incline. I should've known, it would end like that. Mr. McAllister always had a thing for Nathan. I'd known it for a while, but still, I'd defended that fucker.

The anger helped motivate me to get back on the trail. "Well, at least it did some fucking good," I said out loud to the all but silent world around me.

I took a deep breath and exhaled slowly. I needed to get back to the trailhead and off the mountain.

I let the shitshow that was my life continue to play in my mind, hoping the frustration, upset, and horror of it would propel me forward. It was the reason I was out here in the first place, brutally trying to rid myself of my demons through exercise. The physical strain seemed to be just the right cure to forget the idiots back in Seattle, but as my calves burned with each step, sweat poured down my face, and I had to keep stopping to catch my breath, it was also becoming increasingly clear I wasn't in good enough shape to be climbing the Pyramid Peak Trail.

Maybe one of the flatter, shorter hikes would've made more sense. But damn, if the exertion before I fell hadn't felt better than the crap that had taken over my life.

I took another deep breath and let it out slowly, making a concerted effort to focus.

Maneuvering down the path with a broken arm in a makeshift sling made from my backpack was possibly the most difficult thing I'd ever undertaken. The only thing that kept me going was the thought that if I stopped, I'd be eaten by that bear or that if I died a tragic death, it would give Nathan –

that asshole I used to consider a friend – the satisfaction that he might have successfully driven me to my own death.

Nothing, not even the pain or being eaten by a bear, was worse than Nathan thinking I committed suicide because of something he did.

Despite the motivation, I wasn't naïve enough to believe I could make the entire trek back down by myself, although I'd made it to the part of the path that led to the vista. I still knew I had a long way to go. How the hell was I gonna make it out of here?

I could almost kick myself at my own stupidity. *"No problem, I can turn back at any time and head back down the path. It'll be a lot easier going back than it was coming up."*

Those were my very own words. I'm an idiot!

By the time I made it back to a vista I passed on the way up, the sun had gone down, and the temperature was dropping like a lead balloon. Hell, I wouldn't be surprised if it snowed. Despite all my effort, I had reached the end of my ability and my body simply wouldn't take another step. Luckily, the vista had a bench. Bear or not, I had to lie down. I knew my best chances at survival would only come if I stayed on the path in hopes that someone might get the whim to come by and check out the night sky.

My body started to shake, and a cold sweat broke out over me as fear settled in. What the hell was I gonna do? Not one damned soul knew where I was. "Fuck my life!" I hollered out before closing my eyes and giving into my exhausted body.

A fluttering sound above me caught my attention, giving my heart a start that turned into a racing beat.

"Hello?" I yelled out. Seconds later, a large snowy owl landed on the bench next to me.

Why was this bird this far south? I loved nature shows and knew this owl was rare in the park, even in winter.

The fact I was yelling and making a ruckus should've alerted me this was no ordinary owl... much less the fact it wasn't supposed to be here in the summer months.

I remembered my grandmother and I spotting a large barred owl next to her home when I was around eleven years old. That one was staring at me then, much like this one was now.

Grandma was always full of stories from her Native American ancestors. "This owl is a death owl," she'd told me.

Of course, that freaked me out. Was she gonna die, was I gonna die?

She'd laughed. "Not all death is physical, Daniel. Sometimes, it's symbolic of your transitioning. Like now you are transitioning from a boy to a man. This owl has come to celebrate that with you." My grandmother pulled me into a side embrace and whispered into the top of my head, "I think the owl may be one of your guides..."

I shifted on the bench and stared at the beautiful creature in front of me and pondered if this owl was more likely here to transition me from life to death... in a literal sense.

"Hopefully, it'll be fast," I said, and the owl pivoted its head in the strange way owls do and looked down the path.

I was too exhausted to do anything. If I was dying, so be it, I thought, just as I slipped into a deep and restless sleep.

Two

A WOMAN'S SCREAM STARTLED me awake.

"Wha... what are you doing here?" she cried next to me.

I shook the fog out of my head and managed to point to my arm.

"You're injured?" a man, who came running up behind her, asked me.

I nodded. "I fell down the landslide, I've been here all night."

"Oh shit, okay," the man said. "We'll go get help."

I gave them a thumbs up with my good hand. I wanted to hug them, to show them how relieved I was now that someone had found me. I just didn't have the energy.

The cold had been awful and I'm sure I was lucky because hypothermia seemed to be just one or two degrees away.

At least the cold helped soothe the pain in my arm and head a bit. I'd remembered to pack a light blanket in my backpack, which got me through the worst of the cold. I'd managed to get the dammed thing around me sometime in the wee hours of morning, when I'd woken up shivering and surprised I wasn't dead yet. Although, until I was woken by the hikers, I was convinced death was going to be my fate. Had I not made it down to the secluded vista, I'm sure I wouldn't have been so lucky.

The couple returned a short time later with a park ranger who identified himself as Ranger Mike.

"Can you walk, son?" he asked.

Even though I was shivering, and the pain was almost un-bearable, I hadn't lost my smart-ass attitude. Before I could stop myself, I responded, "Sir, if I could walk by myself, I wouldn't be laying here in the cold, would I?"

"No, I suppose not," he said and chuckled. "Well, we have two choices. Either you can wait another thirty minutes or so for the rescue crew to show up, or I can try to help you down to the trailhead. From there, we can get you to a hospital."

I preferred to get down the mountain as soon as possible, so I agreed to his help.

He bandaged my arm against my body, which hurt like a motherfucker; however, once secured, the pain was at least more manageable and a hell of a lot less intense.

With the ranger's help, I shuffled down the path and got about halfway to the trailhead when four guys dressed in white and red uniforms met us.

"You made it here faster than I anticipated," Ranger Mike said to them, clearly surprised.

"Yep," one of them replied. "We were camped out along the ridge ourselves last night."

"Sir," an older man, who looked to be in his fifties, addressed me, "I'm Captain Jones and this is my crew. We're going take you the rest of the way down. Looks like Ranger Mike got you pretty well wrapped."

The men helped me lie down on a stretcher and strapped me in. The pain was still so intense that I closed my eyes and let them do what they wanted. At that point, the only thing going through my head was the desire for pain medication. "Okay, sir, hold on and we'll carry you the rest of the way down."

I was beyond the point of no return. They weren't gonna get any argument out of me. If I had to take another step, I'm sure I would've ended up face down in the dirt.

I was being toted down the hill in jerky movements. I had no idea why or how it happened, but as we were walking down, I suddenly noticed the guy at my left shoulder. He looked down as I looked up and our eyes met. Even though I hurt, and the movements jarred my arm, causing sharp pains to radiate through me, the moment I made eye contact, electrical currents passed through me. Enough to make me forget about the pain for a few moments.

Every ounce of dignity was gone. I was laid bare in front of this man. So, when I got my wits back, I felt nothing less than utter embarrassment. Looking away was the only thing I knew to do, but not before I noticed he'd recognized my attraction for him.

I closed my eyes, refusing to open them again. Even though I thought this whole thing couldn't get worse, I'd shown it could by making eyes with my rescuer. Ugh, I hated my life!

The rest of the trip was uneventful. The rescue squad got me to the main road and I was picked up by an ambulance and taken to a small hospital where my arm was put in a cast. I managed to break the damned thing in five different places. Guess there went my baseball career, not that I ever played baseball.

The medical people in the ER said I was lucky. Just a few months earlier, a hiker had come to a much worse fate on that trail. Had I not gotten down to a more secure position, hypothermia would have been a bigger threat than any of those bears I'd been afraid of.

The staff called my brother, Paul, and he said he was coming to get me. I knew he and his husband Jeff had a gallery opening this coming weekend and I was sure-the-fuck not going to screw that up. So, when he told me he was on his way, I said, "No!" just a little too forcefully. "I'm fine and I still need alone time to figure stuff out in my head. I'll be fine. I've found a hotel just down the road," I lied.

The nursing staff must've heard me, though, because shortly before I was discharged, I was told by one of my favorite nurses that someone had arranged for me to stay in a local B&B while I recovered. It sounded strange, but my cousin was a hospital social worker back in Tennessee, and she'd tell stories of doing similar things for her patients.

Maybe my luck was changing. No, I didn't dare hope that. After I was discharged, an Uber driver picked me up and took me to a bed and breakfast a couple blocks away from the hospital itself.

Someone, I assume one of the rangers, must've packed up my gear and dropped it and my car off where I was staying.

I had just over a thousand dollars to my name and like it or not, I was clearly gonna spend it on recovering from my latest stupid stunt. Not that I was complaining. Had it not been for my situation, I'd be looking at the back of my brother's head, knowing he was disappointed in me. And if I'd had a million bucks, I'd have spent every penny to avoid that.

Three

T HE FIRST TWO DAYS at the bed and breakfast were a haze of painkiller-induced sleep. On the third day, I found myself itching to move around and able to drop the painkillers down a bit.

My host was a short woman with a pixy haircut that had very subtle hints of orange swirled among the salt and pepper named Annabeth. I assumed she was probably in her fifties, although my mom and aunts had taught me early on in life never to ask so I wasn't sure about the last part.

Beth, as she preferred to be called, doted on me as if I were her long-lost son. When I came out of my drug-induced stupor, I asked her why she was so accommodating to a stranger.

"I have a soft spot in my heart for a damsel in distress," she responded.

So much for my anonymity. Guess I should've known folks in these parts would be well enough acquainted with gay men to know one when they saw one.

I didn't know if I'd ever get used to such ways. Where I grew up, the occasional snide comment would slip out of someone's mouth. But, besides those comments or a school bully, no one usually had the nerve to accuse you of being gay to your face.

I remembered hearing my great aunt quote Olympia Dukakis's character in *Steel Magnolias* to describe gay men as men who buttered our toast on the other side.

I guessed that was one of the reasons I loved this part of the country. I liked just being who I was without the sideways glances or the innuendo. I'd never been one for standing out in the crowd. I liked disappearing into the background. I liked a certain amount of anonymity built in, with just an occasional bit of showing off.

Beth was true to her word and treated me like the damsel in distress that I guess I really was. I can't imagine how I would have fed myself, much less kept myself clean, had it not been for her. The attention, at least after I came back to consciousness, began to embarrass me even more. I hated being a burden on such a sweet host.

Luckily, she didn't seem to mind. Beth was a huge fan of the Home Repair Network and especially the show *Space Needle Rehab* with Les Cooper and Bennett Jackson. We bonded as we watched it. She was significantly impressed when I told her Paul and Jeff's friend, Officer Cliff Sparks, had worked with the team on some sort of mess Bennett had gotten wrapped up in. I wasn't sure, but Paul made it out like it had something to do with all the arrests that went down last year.

Unfortunately, I've come to know Officer Sparks a little too well myself through my own drama.

Beth turned the volume up after the commercials ended and Les was back on the screen, muscles gleaming in the camera's lights. He really was a TV god. Bennett was incredibly good looking too, but in a much more dignified and reserved sort of way.

When my brother showed up the following Monday, after his gallery showing, I was happy for the distraction. Beth handed the caretaking reins over to him and even put him up in the room adjoining mine.

"I'm glad you didn't die," he started.

"Me too, I guess," I said, head down.

"Damn you, Daniel, what the hell were you thinking? And why didn't you tell me how seriously injured you were?" His stern voice matched his equally serious and intense expression.

There it was. It wasn't like I didn't know he was gonna lay into me. I guess I was just hoping he wouldn't.

"I didn't want you to miss your gallery showing. You think I didn't know how long you and Jeff had worked on that?"

Paul fumed. "I'm your damned brother and the only family you have around here. Would you have left Mom out of the loop...or Dad?" he huffed and shook his head. "You know if you had, they'd have kicked your ass. Damn if I shouldn't kick it myself!"

"Paul, I didn't want you here. I didn't want *anyone* here. Can't you see that I didn't want to be a bother, that I didn't want to screw anything else up for anyone, especially you?"

I got up, groaning with the effort. I stared out at the pic-turesque view looking out over the sea from my room.

"The trouble with the cops was my fault. I let that... that stupid, shithead fucker get in my head, and the whole falling off the side of a mountain was my fault too. So, enough was enough, I needed to stand on my own two feet and Dad would have approved even if he did kick my ass."

Paul wasn't moved by my speech. "Regardless, you should have at least told me how serious the injury was. How did you get all your gear collected, and who set up this bed and break-fast?"

"I'm not entirely sure. The rangers must've packed me up and brought the car here. I think someone from the hospital set the room before I was discharged. Somehow, it all just fell into place," I chuckled. "It's a small town, the hospital staff must've known Beth was a fag hag, angel of mercy."

Paul stared at me for a long time. I knew he was battling his desire to yell at me. Instead, he shook his head. "Well, despite what you might think, you are one lucky fool. There was a much greater chance that you'd have been left out on the streets to fend for yourself. I guess the fact that you're in a small town did make the difference."

"Yeah, I'm guessing I'm quite the talk of the town as well. Can you imagine what the folks back home would've said about some out-of-town idiot traipsing around getting himself half killed and needing to have the rescue crews bring him out of the forest?"

My brother's serious face finally relaxed, and he chuckled too. "They'd have talked trash about you then blessed your heart up and down fifteen ways to Sunday."

After we'd both had a good laugh, Paul turned back to me and said, in a far gentler voice, "Daniel, I love you, I'm your family, your brother for God's sake. You've gotta stop pushing me away. I know things have sucked for you and you know I've been about as pissed at you as a man can be, but that's only 'cause I want the best for you."

He got up and walked over to the window I'd just left and stared out over the sea.

"Now that Mom and Dad are gone, I feel like it's my responsibility to look out for you. But how the hell am I supposed to do that when you push me to the side and I don't even know you're in trouble until the cops show up at the house?"

I let out a long sigh. "Paul, I don't want you to be responsible for me and that's precisely why I don't tell you all that's going on. You keep trying to be Mom and Dad. Listen, I love you too and I really want you to be proud of me." I wiped a tear before turning to face him. "I hate disappointing you more than anyone I've ever known, but I'm gonna screw up, I have screwed up and... and fuck, Paul, I'm never gonna be perfect."

I shook my head, frustrated, and looked back at Paul. "You put more pressure on me than Mom and Dad ever did. Sometimes it's just too much. I know I haven't tuned out like you thought I should, but I'm not made for college or high-style living. I'm just a regular Joe who happens to be a gay guy. The fact that I'm also a stupid romantic keeps making me trust these idiotic fools, so I end up making bad choices. You married Mr. Perfect. Don't you think it's tough not to have found the same kind of man myself?"

"Daniel, don't be stupid. I'm ten years older than you. Do you think I didn't kiss all the stupid toads before I ran into Jeff?"

He began pacing the room before stopping abruptly and turning back toward me, making eye contact. "We should've had this talk a long time ago," he said.

He was clearly about to launch into the talk when I couldn't stifle a yawn.

"But I can also tell you're getting tired. Hell, I am too. Why don't you rest a bit and I'm gonna go do the same. Let's meet up for dinner. My treat, and I'll tell you about some of the worst toads in my past. There were a lot more than you think."

I nodded, thankful that he was going to give me a break to manage the fatigue that'd just hit me head-on. After he'd left, I popped a pain pill and laid down on the bed. I couldn't even conceive of my high and mighty brother dating my ex, Tony. In fact, the image made me shudder. I wasn't so sure I was ready to hear about his dating past. Paul met Jeff when I was still a teenager, so I'd just always thought that he was his first love. Regardless, he was right. Maybe it was time Paul and I made peace with one another.

I fell asleep before my mind could conjure up any other errant thoughts about my brother's love life. When I woke up a couple hours later, I heard Paul knocking around in his room.

"Time to face the music," I said out loud.

When I came out of my room, I found Paul standing at my door. I could tell he was no more in the mood to share that part of himself than I was to hear it. Good, then I wouldn't be the only uncomfortable one in the conversation.

"Where do you want to eat?" Paul asked.

"I have no idea," I replied. "This'll be the first time I've been anywhere but this bedroom since I got here. Let's ask Beth what she thinks."

Beth's opinion was that we should stick close to the house. In her words, it was unlikely I was gonna feel like doing anything for longer than an hour and if I started to crash, I needed to be able to get back to bed without overdoing it. She recommended a little burger shack about a mile away.

"The food's not great," she said, "but it's quick, cheap and won't give you food poisoning."

The woman had a way with words. She was right though, the burgers tasted like soy and the fries like they'd been picked up from the frozen food aisle at the local grocery store, but she was also correct that my stamina had yet to return to full strength.

I couldn't say I was happy that I'd fallen or broken my arm, but I was glad to have an excuse for the conversation to be kept to a minimum.

"I regret not being closer to you and not confiding in you more. It's just, sharing my life isn't something I've ever been really good at. In fact, if you wanna know the truth, my lack of communication just about kept Jeff and me from ever happening," Paul started.

He sighed and I could tell this was hard for him. "You see, after all the chaos... well, we'll hold off on the details of that for a moment...

"I should have known that opening up to you was gonna be necessary, but, Daniel, we came from the same place, and you know as well as I do how... well, how 'not like us' speaking about our feelings is."

This conversation made me nervous. I wasn't even sure why, but as I freaked out internally at having to have a heart-to-heart with my brother, all I could really do while Paul talked was nod. Yep, this wasn't fun.

"Jeff told me when you first arrived that I needed to open up to you and let you know the real me, the part I kept stored away. I told him that wasn't how we do things where we're from and that you'd probably prefer donating a kidney to having to deal with a brother who was *opening up*. From the look on your face right now, I'm guessing I was right about that, huh?"

"Yep, I'm pondering whether I'll get very far if I run or if I'll just pass out, which honestly might be preferable."

Paul laughed. "Trust me, I feel about the same way. So, let's make this easy. I'm not gonna get sappy but I *am* gonna tell you, your image of me and Jeff is more than a little skewed."

He took a deep breath and then continued. "I was the quintessential lost boy when I first arrived in Seattle. I had a knack for drawing, a degree under my belt and was as green as a lizard lying on a rock. I never liked dating. Hated it, in fact. I'm a backwoods kind of guy and would have been better off finding some guy and shacking up in the hills, but Seattle is no backwoods kind of place. And yes, I know you understand what I'm saying."

He looked at me, a smile on his face. "Several guys came and went in rapid succession. Most of them were better described as clowns and I had about as much interest in pursuing anything with them as I did dating women. So, you can imagine my relief when I met a man who seemed to have culture, liked my art, and was interested in something more than just fucking and drinking."

Paul looked down at his cuticles as he continued speaking.

"The guy was a powder keg. Unbeknownst to me, he was a drug dealer and all-around bad guy. I won't go into the gory details but, not unlike you, I found myself behind bars at one point, had to call Dad to come bail me out and hire me an attorney."

When I looked up in surprise, Paul was staring straight at me.

"Yep, there's the shock I'd have rather never seen on your face," he said as he laughed nervously.

"I wasn't involved in any of the crap that idiot was, but I was guilty by association. My attorney got me off, but not before I cost Mom and Dad a pretty penny. The idiot got life in prison. He damaged me and damaged me bad. I stopped dating and became a recluse. My only goal in life was to pay the parents back. I felt like my fate was to live a lonely existence and end up a nutty old bachelor who died in a one-room cabin. The kind that has one naked light bulb hanging from the center of the ceiling."

I chuckled at the memory of old Mr. Tellerman, who'd lived down the road from us growing up. He literally lived in a one-room cabin with a naked light bulb hanging from the ceiling. He'd also died a millionaire.

"Jeff came into my life at my lowest point," Paul continued. "He owned the competing gallery just down around the corner from the one that'd commissioned my last showing. He stopped by, and I was swept into the current that was his life. Not that I made it easy for him, or me, but we got through the turbulent first years of dating without me running for the hills. The seal on the relationship was when you, Mom and Dad came for your first visit. I don't know if you remember, but Jeff came over for dinner one night. Dad pulled me aside after Jeff left and said, 'That is the one. Don't fuck it up.'" Paul chuckled at the memory before continuing. "Somehow, I didn't. I jumped on the Jeff wagon and never looked back. So, you aren't the only one in our family to screw up. In fact, you aren't even the one to screw up the worst."

He took a long drink of his Mountain Dew.

"I wish you still had Dad here. He would've helped you handle this a lot better than me. But, Daniel, our parents were only able to help me because I let them. No more kicking me to the corner, little brother. Either you're gonna start letting me be a part of your life, or I'm gonna start interfering and meeting your friends and acting like the old Southern diva you know I can be."

He narrowed his eyes and gave me *the* look before releasing a long-suffering sigh. "There are no words to tell you how hurt I am that you fell off a damned mountain, barely survived, and didn't even let me come get you." At that point, Paul, my steel-girded brother, shed the first tear I'd ever seen. I watched it fall from his face and drop onto his shirt. I felt the first real feeling of shame for keeping him out of my life. It hit me square in the gut and I could almost feel our mom's look of disapproval from far beyond the grave.

We both fell silent after that and shortly thereafter, paid and got back into the car to return to Beth's place.

"Paul, I'll make you a promise. Not just for you but for Mom and Dad as well. Even when it's hard and even when I'd prefer to go it alone, I'll make the effort to clue you in. But I need you to do the same for me. I don't need you to be perfect, in fact, I think I needed to see you as you really are. I never saw that side of you before today. Not that I want to get sappy or anything but growing up, you were everything I wanted to be. You were an athlete in high school, had a ton of friends, sang in the church choir. You were my hero. I always knew I'd never stack up to you." I sighed. "I'm guessing the ten-year age gap between us has made you feel more like a parent to me than a brother, so knowing you're human helps too. I really like knowing you were as big a fuck-up as I am."

Thankfully, my injured arm was facing away from him since his punch was instant and unapologetic.

Paul laughed. "Well, don't let it go to your head, I'm still your big brother and I can still kick your butt."

I laughed as well. "I'm at a disadvantage here, or I'd take you up on that challenge."

Paul and I were still laughing as we walked back into Beth's place. We were in a better place than we'd ever been in the past. I guess it made falling off the mountain worth it. Not that I planned to ever do that again.

Paul seemed to know my time here just north of the park wasn't yet done. He lingered for a couple more days, then headed back down to meet Jeff in Seattle. We spent a lot of time over those days laughing about how stupid we'd been with men and about how our Southern family would find this entire scenario hilarious.

We also shared, for the first time, how difficult it had been for both of us to get along without the steady, simple comfort of our parents' support. I'd had no idea he missed them as much as I did. There was comfort in knowing that as well.

Paul didn't try and force me to go back with him when he left, which was a relief. The fact he and Beth worked behind my back to pay for two more weeks was a relief as well, although I'd never have allowed it had I known what they were cooking.

Now, with Paul and Jeff's financial assistance, I was allowed the time to recover both physically and emotionally before I had to go back and face the music.

I'm not sure Paul even understood how valuable that gift really was. I was nowhere close to being ready to face Seattle yet, and sure not ready to face my recent past either. That was gonna come in a few weeks anyway and it was best that I had some time to recover before I was forced to explain my actions to a judge.

Four

My recovery was progressing nicely, and by the end of the third week after the accident, I no longer had to have pain medication just to get through the day. I still sometimes needed it to get through the nights though.

I'd even started venturing out into the yard while Beth did her gardening, and pulling a few weeds with my good hand. Mostly, I hungered for the company. It was on one of our morning gardening adventures that Beth announced the other two rooms next to mine would be occupied for the weekend. Her nephew was staying, and he'd invited a couple friends to spend the weekend as well. They'd been camping in the park and were ready for more 'modern accommodations,' she'd said with a chuckle. They weren't the first guests who'd stayed in the adjoining rooms, so it perplexed me a bit that Beth thought it necessary to inform me. Oh well, maybe it was just small talk to pass the time as we pulled out wild carrot and pigweed.

"Why don't you come down for a late lunch this afternoon and meet them. They've stayed with me before and I think you may find them interesting," she said with a subtle smile.

"Mrs. Beth," I asked warily, "what are you up to?"

"Me?" she asked, putting her hand across her chest like she was a Southern belle. "Nothing, of course. These two are a married couple, so you have nothing to worry your little head about."

"Mrs. Beth, I've not known you long, but I'm almost sure you're scheming something." At that, Beth laughed in a sly way.

"I'm not an interfering kind of woman. If you don't want to come meet them, there's no one twisting your arm."

"No, no, I'm happy to come down and meet your new guests. Besides, who would turn down a free meal?"

"Who indeed?" She laughed and winked at me.

I went back to my room and began clicking around on my computer, trying to avoid anything to do with my ex-friend Nathan Shit Face, or any of his cronies. I'd unfriended and blocked both him and my ex-boyfriend Tony the night I was released from jail.

Despite my efforts, however, I hadn't deleted everyone on my Facebook page that knew Nathan and Tony. As I read down my feed, I ran across a picture of the two of them kissing. Well, I could have lived the rest of my life without seeing that picture. I blocked the woman who posted it, erasing the picture from my feed.

The gut-punch was more about seeing the betrayal of a so-called friend. Honestly, I didn't give a damn about Tony. He wasn't gonna last much longer anyway.

The only consolation was that the pictures showed Nathan's nose was still red and swollen. I guess a few weeks in the county jail might be worth that punch after all.

I looked over at the clock and noticed it was the afternoon. It was time I went down and found out what Beth was cooking up, both metaphorically and physically. I walked into the kitchen to find her all aflutter. Patsy Cline was wailing in the background about going out after midnight, and Beth was totally in her element. I was lucky to have landed in this incredible woman's home. I was sure Beth and I were bound to be lifetime buddies. I walked into the room, startling her.

"Daniel, what are you doing skulking around? I told you one o'clock, not twelve-thirty," she said.

I shrugged.

"I came down to see if I could offer any assistance. Besides, I'm tired of my own company."

"Well," she said, "turn down that music over there and I'll see if I can't put you to work."

That she did. I was in charge of placing the sandwiches she'd cut up onto porcelain trays along with small, sweet treats and other party favors.

"Who the hell are these guys, Mrs. Beth? It looks like you're preparing tea for royalty."

"Oh, honey, you should know by now that I never miss an opportunity to entertain queens."

"Mrs. Beth, you are a piece of work. How did you get to be so gay savvy?"

Beth roared a delighted laugh and said, "Oh, baby, I've been around gay men since college. I grew up here and went to Berkeley in the early seventies. By the time I got there, San Francisco was the gay mecca and I absolutely loved being right in the middle of it all."

She winked at me. "One of my best friends lived right down in the Castro District and he had the most beautiful brother I'd ever seen. I ended up marrying the man. He and I settled up here a few years after we both graduated. I had so many friends back then..." she shook her head and almost to herself said, "until the AIDS epidemic of the eighties took most of them from us. My heart still breaks over that."

I frowned. The AIDS crisis still affected us, but not like it used to. "What happened to your husband? I've never heard you mention him before."

"Oh, my beautiful William... Well, about five years ago he got sick with leukemia. Lost him just a few months after he was diagnosed. That's when I decided to open the bed and breakfast. I wasn't in any mood to live in this rambling old house all by myself and I don't like people enough to live with them permanently, so the ebb and flow of guests is the perfect life for me."

Beth rushed off into the living room before I had a chance to ask any more questions. I could have kicked myself for upsetting her, especially when she'd been so happy about her queen party. I grabbed the pitcher of lemonade she'd made and followed in her wake.

"Daniel, you have a seat now, and I'll get the rest of this stuff in. The boys should be arriving any moment and I don't want you worn out before they get here." She swept over to give me a kiss on the cheek. Yep, I was lucky to have landed in this incredible woman's home.

Just as Beth left the room, the front door popped open. I saw luggage, and then Beth grabbed up into a bear hug as arms and bodies piled through the opening. Two men came around the corner and Beth turned and pointed to an area next to her sofa for the guys to put their luggage.

"You boys just put your stuff there for the time being. We can sort all that out later. For now, I want to introduce you to my other guest, Daniel Porter."

She dashed into the room, and I greeted them with a smile.

"Daniel, this is Mac and Todd. Did I get that right?" When they nodded their heads in agreement, she continued, "Mac, Todd, this is Daniel. Y'all just make yourselves comfortable. Joseph," she called out to someone who hadn't made it into the house yet, "go on out and get the rest of the luggage. I'll manage the refreshments."

Mac and Todd came over and sat down on the sofa across from me after shaking my good hand. "I hear you had quite a fall over in the park."

"Yeah," I groaned. "That's what I get for going on a sullen adventure without doing adequate research, I'm afraid."

The men nodded agreement, mostly I thought to be friendly, and I was glad they didn't dig too much more into the subject.

"We've been hiking and camping in and around the western part of the park. The coast is what we came up for, and the fishing, of course," Todd said.

"Of course," I repeated, as if I knew anything about fishing. I could have counted on the fingers of my good hand the number of gay men I personally knew who'd find fishing a fun option, much less think of it as an *of course*. But the two seemed friendly enough and I turned toward them to ask where they hiked when the other member of the party walked into the room.

The gut-punch of lust hit first, followed by a familiar embarrassment when I recognized him. I found myself looking into the face of the same guy who had helped carry me down the mountain just a few weeks earlier. Oh shit...

I gawked, red-faced, and what must have been an hour passed as I tried to find the composure to get myself out of the room before I passed out. Beth came to my rescue.

"Daniel, honey, are you okay? You look like you just saw a ghost. Why don't you come with me and I'll get you back to your room." She took me by the good hand and led me out of the room, fussing as we went. "I was afraid we'd push you too far today. I warned you." Bless her ever-loving heart. I was able to nod an embarrassed look at the three men before escaping.

When I got back to my room, I immediately began packing. Yes, I was a coward, and yes, this coward was hightailing it out of here before I had to face that beautiful man and my utter humiliation again. I'd just turned to grab the last of my clothes when I heard a knock at the door.

"Daniel, honey, can we come in?" *Shit, shit, shit!* There was no way out. I owed Beth more than running away anyway.

"Yes, just give me a minute." I closed the drawers and my bag and stuffed it back under the bed. "Okay, come on in."

Beth came in first, followed closely by my very, *very* handsome rescuer. "Daniel, this is my nephew, Joseph. I see the two of you have met before. Had I known you'd remembered him, I would never have surprised you like that. I'm beyond apologetic. Now, Joseph, you have something to share?"

He cleared his throat. "Yes, um... Yes, I do." He looked at me, and I saw concern etched across his face. "I know it's a bit awkward to meet people who rescued you, but you were hurt so bad when we last met that I had no idea you'd remember me. Had I known, like my Aunt B, I'd have never put you in this position. I'm very sorry for the shock."

Two sets of eyes landed on me, and I was left with nothing to do other than sit down on the bed and let them both off the hook. It didn't hurt that both of them looked genuinely concerned.

"I... I also apologize for my rude behavior with you and your friends. They must think I'm a total idiot."

"No," Joseph assured me. "At the moment, the only person they think is an idiot is me."

"A feeling shared among many at the moment," Beth added.

With a sideways glance at his aunt, Joseph added, "If you prefer, I'll be happy to stay somewhere else. I don't want to make you uncomfortable."

Uncomfortable. The fact that the man melted me with one look like a stick of butter in a hot frying pan is what made me uncomfortable. Add to it that while he was hauling my lame ass down a mountain, I was making googly eyes at him. That wasn't uncomfortable. That was downright bury me under a toadstool unbearable.

Despite that, I heard myself say, "Oh. No, no, don't be silly, I'm just embarrassed that I had to be toted down a mountain like a disobedient child. That's my own stupid pride and I will put that where it belongs. If anyone is going to leave, that would be me."

"The hell you will," Beth stepped up. "I'll not hear any more of that nonsense, young man. You are paid up and you'll be staying right here, even if I have to call your brother and get him here to help me tie you down."

With that, the ice was broken and all three of us broke into a laugh.

"I'll be fine, I promise, Mrs. Beth. And there is no need to get my big brother involved. Where I'm from, embarrassment is fodder for a better set of stories to tell over Christmas."

"Well," she said, "that's settled, then. Joseph, come help me get things put back together for our luncheon. I'm starved, and I am not about to let all that food go to waste. Daniel, honey, if you think you're up to it, we'd love to have you join us."

"Yes, ma'am," I said. "I'll be out in just a moment. I need to do a couple things here, though, before I join you."

She nodded and disappeared out the door. Joseph lingered and looked back at me. "I really had no idea you'd remember me. I feel like a total jackass for dragging you through this. Maybe I can make it up to you while you're here."

I smiled and nodded. With that, he slipped out of my room.

It was gonna be an interesting weekend. "God, help me get through this without making a bigger fool of myself," I prayed.

Somehow, I had the feeling that my prayer was gonna go unanswered. When it came to the jaw-dropping gorgeous nephew Joseph, there was no way I was gonna avoid looking like a blubbering fool, never mind my unfortunate trip down the mountain.

I unpacked my clothes, thankful I had the good sense to hide the fact that I'd packed in the first place. I harbored no doubt that Beth's statement about getting my brother involved was not an empty threat. Best if no one knew I had even considered leaving.

Besides, now that I'd overcome the initial shock, the thought of sleeping next door to a dark, handsome man like Joseph was one I was beginning to relish. Even if there was a wall between us.

I stepped into the living room just as Beth poured another round of lemonade for her guests.

"Shall I pour you a glass, Daniel?" she asked when she saw me.

"Yes, please, and I'd love a couple of those lady sandwiches." I heard myself becoming more formal. I tended to switch to my mother's early childhood training of good manners when I was in an impossible position. Beth must've picked up on it too 'cause she grinned and winked at me, then handed me a small china plate rimmed with gold and covered in pink flowers.

As I filled the plate with the dainty sandwiches, I launched into the question I'd intended to ask Mac and Todd before I'd seen Joseph.

"I believe, at least until I became a speechless ninny, that you were going to tell me where you had camped."

Mac smiled. "We camped in several sites, but mostly we were there to fish."

"That's right, you said that. So, not to be rude, but you're the first *male* gay couple I've met that fish." They both chuckled and confirmed that they didn't know many themselves.

"This is why we hang out with guys like Joseph. He may not be a fisherman, but he does know the outdoors. His knowledge of the park has given us access to hidden places we would never have found on our own."

"Joseph, I have to admit, I don't know much about you other than you have the ability to haul unfortunate tourists off mountain trails when they're foolish enough to need such things."

Joseph blushed a little, causing a strange sensation to warm my body all over. He was rather adorable when he blushed.

"I'm on the rescue squad, and I'm a seasonal ranger for the park. I grew up in these parts, so I've spent my whole life navigating the trails, both hidden and known. As far as unfortunate tourists go, I wouldn't be too hard on yourself for needing our services. You were quite brave up there. You did the right thing securing your arm and getting down to the lower elevation. You impressed all of us."

It was my turn to blush and I'm sure I did with gusto. Once again, I was saved by Beth's return to the room.

"Did I ever tell you how I took a tumble on the Pyramid Peak Trail?" she asked, and Joseph looked over at his aunt with concern.

"No, I don't recall you ever telling that story," Joseph said with a raised eyebrow.

"Well, I did, and it sounds like my fall took place about the same location Daniel's did," she said.

The transition Joseph underwent from concerned nephew to professional was instant.

"They really need to do some work on that old trail," he said.

"I heard they're meeting about that in the next few weeks. I'm guessing Daniel's tumble might just have been the straw to break the camel's back, and before you get all tore up about this Daniel, it may be the thing to save another life. Several lives even. Folks around here know how nasty that pass can be and even knowing how dangerous it is, we could still take a tumble. The fact that our tourists have no idea how dangerous that pass is, makes it pure negligence," Beth continued.

I really wanted to get off that topic before it inevitably came back to me and my idiotic lack of preparedness, so I changed the subject. "Mac, Todd, where do you two live?"

"Oh, we live in Edmonds, just north of Seattle," Mac replied.

"Yeah, I know it well," I said smiling. "I live with my older brother, Paul, and his husband in Edmonds as well. Have you taken the ferry over to Kingston?" I asked, knowing it would be strange if they hadn't. "Sometimes Paul and I go over just to get an ice cream, then we ride back."

"That area is beautiful, and I understand why you enjoy the ride. We do the ice cream run ourselves from time to time. So, your brother is gay as well?" Todd asked.

"Yeah, it kind of runs rampant in my family, which makes my very religious, conservative Tennessee relatives a bit edgy."

Todd chucked. "I'm sure it does. I'm originally from Oklahoma, and that subject is avoided at all costs in my neck of the woods."

"No doubt." I shook my head. "I'm lucky, though. My uncle broke the ice when he came out in the late eighties. So, Paul and I came out to a relatively easy-to-manage family."

"Do you still have contact with them?" Mac asked.

"Oh, yeah," I chuckled. "Maybe a little too much contact. My folks passed away a few years back, and I moved out here to live with Paul and his husband. My grandparents were in no way happy about it, as they said we would end up ruining the family name as we went, and I quote, *'cattin' around all over Washington state.'* My grandparents don't quite get what the whole gay thing means. In their minds, it's just wild sex parties with whoever is available at the time."

Joseph snickered. "Sounds fun."

"Well, the apple doesn't fall far from the tree with respect to Paul and me. We run a little more on the conservative side of the gay experience. Paul got hooked up with his husband while I was still in high school, and I'm not much for the promiscuous lifestyle either."

Beth chuckled and, with another of her telling winks, said, "So you're the marrying kind of guy."

"No, I can't say I'm doing a very good job at that either. I was up on that trail, working through a pretty nasty breakup. I'm more of the gonna grow old sitting on the front porch of a shack with a shotgun on one side and a hound dog laying on the other, kind of guy."

The entire room laughed.

"How old are you, Daniel, twenty-five, twenty-six? You got a few years before that future comes to pass. Besides, men are a lot like a good bottle of wine. It takes a few years of maturing before you know if you have a good one or if he's just an old bitter bottle of vinegar," Beth retorted.

"Damn, Mrs. Beth," I added, "you sure have a way with words."

Joseph chuckled in his lemonade. "You have *no* idea, absolutely *no idea*."

I looked over just in time to see Beth give Joseph a warning glance and for Joseph to flash a broad smile before taking a sip of lemonade. That look was enough to confirm my initial suspicion that there's more to Beth than meets the eye. I resolved then and there to get to the bottom of the mystery in the time I had left.

"Hey," Todd looked over at Mac, then to Joseph, "Daniel, do you think you're up to going back into the woods for a little fishing expedition tomorrow? We were just talking on the way over that we'd like to get a few more hours in before we head back to the city."

"Daniel, I don't mean to speak for you, but I'm not sure you should be back out hiking a trail just yet. Doc's orders were to keep you rested for more time than you've had," Beth chimed in before I had a chance to even open my mouth.

"I agree," Joseph said. "It may be a bit early for hiking through the woods but since we're only going to be on the edge of the lake and there's minimal hiking to get to where we're setting up, I can't see why it'd hurt. And I promise if he starts getting tired, I'll bring him right back here."

Todd looked back over at me and asked, "So you up for another adventure?"

"Why the hell not," I said. "What difference does it make sitting here or sitting there. Just as long as you guys understand, I'll be a lump on a log and I have no plans of sticking an innocent worm on any hooks."

Mac smiled. "We don't do that kind of fishing here. We fly fish mostly."

With an involuntary grin, I replied, "Sounds good to me then."

The rest of the afternoon was uneventful. Mac and Todd did a lot of talking about their favorite hobby and the places they'd been to do it. Joseph was mostly quiet, listening to the stories of his two friends. Beth swooped in and out as the afternoon turned into evening. By dinnertime, I was famished.

"Shall I order a pizza?" I asked.

Beth bustled back in. "Absolutely not. I've got dinner pretty much done. We are having an old-fashioned meatloaf, mashed potatoes and gravy, and a side of green beans."

Joseph looked up and inquired, "When did you have time to do that?"

"Oh, I didn't. I called down to the local supermarket and they're bringing it by any moment. Why would I dirty up my kitchen when the girls down at the market have already mussed up theirs? Seems a waste to me."

We all chuckled and in a short time, true to her word, there was a knock at the door and a good ol' fashioned meal appeared before us. My host's skills to entertain were really beginning to impress me.

We all ate like we hadn't eaten in weeks and talked the rest of the evening away, and by nine, I was ready for bed.

"Gentlemen, it has been entertaining, but if I'm gonna be up with the chickens so I can get down to y'all's fishing hole, then I better turn in," I said, getting up from the chair.

"Yeah," Mac agreed, "we better all start heading that way. Mrs. Beth, you sure we can't talk you into joining us tomorrow?"

"No," she said, shaking her head. "My fishing days are over. I'll be spending the day down at the beauty parlor getting ready for you handsome boys to return. Now, don't eat anything on your way home. I've got a surprise in store for tomorrow night's dinner."

"Nobody can argue with a free meal, Mrs. Beth," Todd said.

With that, we all headed to our rooms. I brushed my teeth, got undressed and fell asleep the moment my head hit the pillow. Of course, my mind had just enough time to reflect back on the day and that ridiculously handsome face of Joseph's. Yep, I was for sure gonna enjoy tomorrow and seeing that hunk of a man in his element.

Five

I woke up just before my alarm went off on my phone and rolled over to a pretty serious ache. Damn, I'd forgotten to take anything for the pain last night. I sure as hell hoped it didn't keep me from going out. I did wonder if maybe I should cancel anyway. No way did I want a repeat of Sir Joseph sweeping me up and hauling my delicate ass back to safety. Or, maybe I secretly did... but I wasn't gonna let that happen and face another bout of embarrassment.

I decided to give myself a little time and headed toward the bathroom to get ready. I walked out of my room and right into the arms of Joseph.

"Umm... morning," Joseph said.

I looked up and, for the third time, found myself speechless by the sheer lust that the look of this guy stirred in me. I caught my breath.

"We really need to stop meeting this way," I joked.

The stubble on his cheek rubbed against my forehead before he was able to step away. "I'm guessing we were headed to the same place. Go ahead. I'll use the one down the hall. I'm sure Aunt B won't mind if I share hers to get ready."

"Of all of us, you're probably the only one who can get away with such a thing."

"You know my aunt pretty well after just a few weeks. That's good. It'll keep you alive for your remaining ones," he said chuckling.

"That's probably true," I said, although I couldn't imagine why I'd ever be afraid of Beth. Before I left, I turned back. "Hey, Joseph. I should've taken something for the pain last night, and since I didn't, I'm feeling pretty uncomfortable. Do you think the guys will be too disappointed if I take a raincheck on today?"

"Not at all. It's best for you to take care of yourself and heal properly. There's plenty of time for us all to go fishing when you recover," he said and gave me a warm smile.

I returned the smile and thanked him for understanding.

Did he really say for us all to go fishing *after* I recover? I wondered if he realized I was only booked at the bed and breakfast for a little more time before I had to head back to the city to face the music.

Well, I knew he didn't know about the court stuff, but the leaving part? I thought he should have expected that. I also thought about how long I could survive without an income?

Maybe he thought his benevolent aunt was putting me up as a charity case. That was something to clear up as soon as possible. I may have been an idiot tourist that got himself injured on the top of a dangerous trail and required rescuer intervention, but

I sure as hell was no mooch. Sexy man or not, I needed to make that clear the first chance I got.

The guys left around five in the morning and I went back to bed after popping a much-needed dose of Ibuprofen. I woke up around nine-thirty to bustling and banging somewhere in the house. I slipped some clothes on and wandered out of my room to find Beth surprised to see me still there.

"Yeah," I said in response to the look of surprise she gave me. "I had a rough night and decided to take it easy today."

"I'm glad to hear that," she said. "I thought it was too early for you to be getting out anyway. I did promise your brother I'd watch out for you while you were here."

"Aaaah, I figured there was some conspiracy between the two of you. Now you've confirmed it."

"You caught us," she said with a wave of her hand. "We both want you to stay healthy and out of trouble."

"What's up with all the noise?" I asked.

"Oh, honey, I didn't think. I'm sorry I woke you up. When I heard the house was going to be empty, I called my brother-in-law and asked him to come over and fix a couple things while you were away. I can send him off, but if I do we won't be having any more food prepped for us. They have my whole kitchen in shambles."

"No, I like food," I said. "And the noise isn't bothering me." I turned just in time to see a tall, dark-skinned man with Joseph's eyes walk out of the kitchen.

"Now, who might this be?" he asked.

"Kaden, this is my guest, Daniel Porter. Daniel, this is Kaden McCoy, my brother-in-law and Joseph's father."

"Nice to meet you, Mr. McCoy," I said, sticking out my good hand.

"Likewise," he said, shaking it. "I've heard some good things about you. Joseph said you were smarter than the average bear out on that trail. You impressed him."

"That makes one of us then," I said mournfully.

Kaden repeated his son's words about not beating myself up too much. "That pass is an abomination and needs to have some serious work done to it before it can hurt anyone else," he said.

"I appreciate your kind words and it is becoming apparent that most folks here aren't too keen on the old pass. It's really a beautiful place, at least until I took my fall. I was happy it wasn't the place I died, but at one point I did think at least if I gotta die, I'm dying in a place worthy of haunting."

"Maybe," he said. "But those mountains have plenty ghosts and we don't need to be adding yours to the mix." With that, he headed back outside to get more supplies for the kitchen remodel.

"I'm just about to head down to the supermarket for breakfast and some coffee that doesn't have sawdust in it. You up to joining me?" Beth asked.

"Sure," I said. "Just give me a second to change and brush my teeth."

"You might have a swipe at that cute mop of hair too, while you're at it. If I'm going to be seen around town with a boy on my arm, I'd like him to look his best."

"Sure thing, Mrs. Robinson," I chuckled. "I'll be out in just a second."

Beth giggled at the reference, seeming to appreciate the cougar analogy, and turned toward her own part of the house.

It took me a little bit longer than a second to get ready. I kept forgetting that maneuvering my arm was no easy feat and clothing it was even worse. I came back out about thirty minutes later to Beth and Kaden in a pretty involved conversation.

I considered turning back into my room when Beth spotted me. "It's about time. I thought I was going to have to send in the cavalry."

"Sorry," I said. "Still getting used to how much time this damned arm requires."

"Oh, well, I should have thought of that myself," she said, understanding. "Anyway, I'm hungry enough to start gnawing on the plywood here and I'm about ten minutes from a caffeine headache from my lack of coffee this morning."

She sent a pointed look at Kaden, who just shrugged and replied, "You said it had to be done today."

"And I meant it," she said.

"Meanwhile, don't you forget what I just told you and I expect you will be doing something about it."

"I expect you do. Now get your interfering self out of my way or else this *won't* be done today."

Once we were outside, I asked, "What was all that about?"

"Oh, that's nothing. Kaden lost his wife about ten years ago and has refused to even consider another woman. Not that I can blame him, Joseph's mother was one fine woman and not hard on the eyes either. But last month, this pretty nurse started working down at the hospital and Kaden bumped into her while his company was doing some renovations for them.

"From what I hear through the grapevine, it was love at first sight for both of them, but Kaden is worried that sparking up a relationship with a new woman will upset his son." She shook her head. "So, my stubborn brother-in-law is avoiding getting involved... or at least he's *trying* to avoid it."

She looked over at me and winked. "This nurse of his doesn't seem to be willing to take no for an answer."

"I can't really blame her. Mr. McCoy is one mighty good-looking man. If it wasn't for the fact he was twice my age and straight, I'd be pretty keen myself."

Beth looked at me smiling. "You are bold this morning," she retorted, then laughed.

"Oooh, things are beginning to clear up. Your husband you mentioned, but wait... I thought the brother was gay."

"He was... is... Evan is William's twin and Kaden's *older* brother. He lives down in Portland these days, running a clinic. He works with the Native American population there."

"I see. How many brothers does this family have?" I asked, genuinely interested.

"Just the three and an older sister as well. She lives just around the corner, and it's a miracle she hasn't been over to the house since you arrived. I'm sure you'll meet her before it's all said and done." Her face became suddenly serious. "But I warn you, Martha is a force to be reckoned with."

"Do you have siblings?" I asked.

"Me? No, I'm an only child. My parents were only married a couple years before they split up and went their separate ways. I was raised by my grandparents in the house I still live in now."

Beth parked the car and we walked into the supermarket, then directly over to the café. "We'll have two coffees, Mary," she said upon walking in, "and Daniel here will have his with cream and sugar."

"Right away, Mrs. Clemens."

"Clemens?" I asked, confused. "If you married a McCoy, how are you a Clemens?"

"Now, don't get all private investigator on me. I didn't change my name when William and I got married. You have to remember, our wedding occurred in nineteen eighty-four, just as the feminist movement was getting its groove on. I fancied myself a feminist, still do really, and I couldn't see any benefit in casting off my name when it seemed to fit me fine. William's family weren't too pleased, but there wasn't much they could do."

She chuckled at the memory. "He and I were about as stuck on each other as anybody could be but I was as bull-headed then as I am now. There wasn't much they could do besides grin and bear it. Which is precisely what his poor mother did."

When the woman behind the counter placed our coffees down, Beth turned her attention to her. "Mary. Now that you've got us some coffee, why don't you mix me up some eggs, bacon and a biscuit, like I usually get? Daniel, you haven't been here long enough to have a usual so, what would you like?"

"Oh, just a biscuit would be fine. My stomach is still a bit queasy this morning." The young waitress nodded in a rush and went back to place the order.

We crossed over to a table and had just sat down when Beth asked, "Now tell me, why didn't you go with the boys this morning? You said you weren't feeling up to it. Do I need to call over to the clinic and get you back in?"

"Oh, no. Nothing like that. We had so much fun last night I forgot to take any painkillers before going to bed. I woke up with a little more pain than I was ready to tackle. So, I rainchecked, took some Ibuprofen and headed back to bed. I'm doing fine now and won't repeat that mistake again tonight, I assure you."

We finished our breakfast and Beth asked if I wanted to join her at the beauty shop. When she saw me cringe, she laughed. "If you prefer, you can always go back to the construction site I call home."

In the most delicate Southern drawl I could imagine, I said, "Mrs. Beth, there is no man in his right mind, gay or straight, who would walk into the lion's den of the local beauty shop when he has just breezed into town. They'd have me filleted and served on cucumber sandwiches before your hair's been set."

She giggled. "You are wise beyond your years. I'll take you back to the house and you can keep an eye on that brother-in-law of mine. I'll expect a report on whether he's getting that pantry floor put in or lollygagging around waiting on that little nurse to call."

I cocked my eyebrow at her. "I'm sure Mr. McCoy is competent enough without my interference. I'm gonna get on to the computer and let my brother know I'm still alive and functioning. If I don't, we can expect he'll put in another surprise visit come Monday."

"That wouldn't be a problem for me, young man," Beth said, her naughty personality coming to the surface once again. "Your brother is quite easy on the eyes. I have no problem with him coming to stay anytime he likes."

I choked as we pulled into the driveway. "Okay, this conversation is too much for me. I'm going in and forgetting your wiggly eyebrows and comments about my brother." I closed the door to her laughter and saw Kaden rounding the corner.

"Back already, huh. I see you decided to forgo the hen party at the beauty shop."

"Merciful God, yes. I learned from my mama's beauty parlor there is nothing more dangerous than a group of women getting their hair done."

Kaden laughed. "Son, you are smarter than you look."

"Thanks," I said shrugging. "I guess."

Kaden looked at me for a moment. "Since you're here, how about you hold this plywood while I cut it down to size. I know you've only got one hand, but that's all I need."

I appreciated the change from Beth's teasing to the solid, stoic company of Kaden, so I gladly accepted.

I helped Kaden and his crew, as much as I could with a broken arm, through the rest of the morning and into the afternoon. The wife of one of the guys had packed an extra sandwich so that even took care of lunch. I'd forgotten how much I liked working on a construction site. My dad, uncles, and grandfather were always building or fixing something on the farm, and the steady hum of the multitude of power tools always put me at ease.

By the time Beth came back from her hair appointment, I was ready for a break. The kitchen complete, with the exception of the cleanup, which Kaden said was Beth's part of the arrangement, I tucked into the shower before the guys returned.

After my shower, I came out to the sound of Beth's barely contained excitement as she showed the cabinet to the guys. "You see, it has those fancy adjustable shelves and curves so beautifully. I also love the tiger maple we picked out. Don't those lines just make you want to cry? All it needs is a coat of poly and it'll be here a hundred years from now."

Beth was bursting at the seams to show off her new built-in china cabinet to her nephew. Truth was, I was surprised at Kaden and his crew's carpentry skills. I was also shocked at how fast the project came together. When I mentioned as much, one of the guys told me that Kaden and his late wife used to operate a furniture shop in Seattle before he retired and moved back to these parts.

Mac and Todd just smiled at her and ooh'd and aah'd appropriately. Beth accepted their nods as interest and continued. "I hated that old shelf I had. Been here since I was a girl, and it was wobbly and useless. My grandmother should have used the thing for firewood fifty years ago." Then Beth turned toward me and said, "I guess there are always things we need to toss to the curb but still hold onto for whatever reason. For me, I'm glad to have traded the garbage for a jewel."

That made me wonder if Beth knew more about my situation than she'd let on? I hadn't told her, and I seriously doubted no-nonsense Paul would have shared anything about other people's business even when he was pissed.

Growing up in the South with all the strong women in my family, I'd learned quickly there was little they couldn't naturally sniff out. Beth might not know the details, but she seemed to know enough to make me squirm.

Mac and Todd excused themselves and headed into the shower to wash off their day while Joseph, Beth, Kaden and I all moved into the living room.

"Dad said you helped him with some of the work on the cabinet."

"Yeah," I said. "If you call it that. With one arm, mostly I was just in the way."

Kaden contradicted me. "I suspect you'd be pretty handy if you had both hands. You were actually a big help. My grunt worker called in sick. Sounds like he's got this flu that's been sweeping the countryside. You never know how much you need a grunt until you don't have him."

I laughed. "Well, sir, I have many years' experience in the 'grunt department.' I don't reckon you live on a farm and not get used to running errands when someone needs you to."

"Have you ever worked in construction?" Beth asked.

"Well, not officially," I responded. "But as I said before, I grew up on a farm and we were always building or tearing something down. I was thinking today how much I missed the work. Brought back some pleasant memories of my dad."

Kaden chimed in before the familiar sadness set in. "Well, son, I know you're on vacation, but I need another grunt, and one hand or not, you proved yourself useful today. I'd be happy to put you on my team until my other guy gets back on his feet."

"You sure I wouldn't be more of a hindrance than a help?"

"Son," Kaden replied, "I'll make a deal with you. If you become a hindrance, I'll send ya packing. How does that sound?"

I shrugged with a chuckle. Kaden reminded me so much of my own father. "Sounds fair to me," I said, knowing the threat wasn't an idle one. "I'd welcome the distraction and I'm almost sure Beth would like her house back from the infirm."

"That is a bunch of nonsense, child. I've really enjoyed taking care of someone besides myself for a change. That being said, if you take it easy, I do think it would do you good to be out doing something besides sitting around a house with an old woman."

"Oh, Mrs. Beth, I don't know, I've been pondering whether I should pop the question."

"Boy," she replied, "you'd make mighty fine arm candy, *but*..." She made a point of looking at Joseph then back at me. "I think there are those out there that'd enjoy your candy a bit more than me."

Oh, that woman. I felt my face flush at the comment. And since Beth had so eloquently put me in my place, there was nothing I could do other than nod and say, "I do love to share my candy." Beth and Kaden laughed, but I noticed that Joseph just smiled and blushed a shade lighter than me.

"If you're serious, I'll pick you up Monday morning at eight sharp. I have a project I agreed to do for the local butcher shop. Seems they need some shelves built for a new display. It's a one-man job but I tend to get caught up in the moment and need someone to man the phone and deal with any issues that come up. You able to do that?" Kaden asked.

"Yes, sir, I'll be ready at eight."

I let myself get talked into Mac and Todd's fishing trip the next day and remembered to take my Ibuprofen the night before, so when the morning came, I was up, ready, and pain-free. Apparently, their Saturday catch had been above average, so they forwent their plans to move to a different spot for one more day on the lake.

Honestly, I went just because I wanted an excuse to spend a little more time looking at Joseph. If I were to guess, he had to be about six foot three, which meant he towered over my own five foot eleven. Everything about Joseph melted my butter. Tall, slender, and skin the color of warm caramel. I did love licking caramel, I thought to myself as we drove toward the fishing spot. Todd and Mac were in the back seat chatting away, occasionally asking Joseph questions, which allowed me to just spend time in my own head.

I quickly glanced over at him and noticed his above-average-sized bicep. *I loved a nice-sized bicep.* Oh, but the thing that had caused me to melt from the moment I first saw him was his slightly larger than they should have been brown eyes. Every feature on his face seemed to be made to accentuate those eyes.

I turned my attention back toward the road then glanced back over to see if I could catch another glimpse of his handsome face just in time to see him wink at me. I felt my face heat and I quickly turned my attention back out the front window.

I'm not what you would call an eye man. Usually, I'm all about the butt, but on this particular fella it was all about those eyes. The guy had made me speechless with just one look, including when I was managing the worst, most excruciating pain I'd ever encountered.

Even before I'd seen Joseph the second time, I couldn't quite get the picture of his face out of my mind. I had incorrectly assumed he was some straight guy volunteering on a back-woods rescue team, but I admit it was unusual for me to react so strongly to a straight guy. I luckily had some kind of gaydar thing built into my attraction that kept me from falling for a man who couldn't return my feelings.

I laid my head back on the seat and closed my eyes, remembering when I'd first seen him. While drifting in and out of consciousness, I kept seeing those eyes looking down at me. The persistent thought was how insanely embarrassing it was to have him haul me down off the mountain, unbathed, half dead, and looking anything but attractive.

If I'd known he was gay at the time, I'd have given up any hope of him ever looking my way again. Finding out he was Beth's nephew, well, that was a shock to the system that I wouldn't quite get over. I thought it was fishy I ended up there, but I hadn't had the nerve to find out what, if any, influence he had in my post-injury housing.

I decided to stamp down my pride and just see where things went. I suspected Beth's candy comments wouldn't have made him blush the night before had he not at least had some interest in me. That being said, I didn't expect too much. He must have still had an image of me sprawled out helpless on a stretcher on that dreaded ass trail. Regardless, he was at least nice to be with, even if his love interests were minimal. I was happy with that. Besides, attracted to me or not, he still occasionally looked at me with those amazing eyes.

When we finally arrived, Joseph stationed me in a very comfortable chair while he and the guys set up their gear to fly fish. After Mac and Todd were set, Joseph excused himself and headed down to the ranger station to, as he said, "check-in."

What he was checking in on, I didn't ask, since I'm sure it was something to do with making sure some nitwit city slicking hiker hadn't fallen off another mountain.

I sat back and watched the two anglers sport their craft. I'd seen fly fishing a few times in my life, but never anything as beautiful as these two. They spent most of their time a dozen or more feet apart, but despite the distance, they were almost always in sync with the other's movements. I wondered if the two of them knew that they danced virtually in rhythm with each other.

During one of their breaks, I asked how long they'd been together, and with a smile, the two informed me they had been together for just over three years. They'd only lived together for one year, though. There was no doubt there was love between them, although it was more subtle than that of my brother and brother-in-law. Mac and Todd seemed more like two best friends who happened to have fallen in love. Everything about the two of them portrayed marital bliss.

I'd always longed for a best friend. In school, I'd been a little too odd for long-term friendships, and with all the work on the farm after Paul left, I really didn't get involved in sports, so the things that connected kids were really not a part of my life.

I often thought that if Paul had been closer to my age, we would've been better friends, but as it was, he was more a third parent than a friend.

So mostly, I'd learned how to be a loner. Although I hated to think about it, that's probably why I was so upset when I saw Nathan kissing Tony. I had finally found a buddy I thought was gonna fill that void, but boy did I ever miss that mark. I knew there were signs. He was always fighting for attention when we were out and he seemed to dismiss me the second any guy he thought was handsome came into his sights. But, when it was just the two of us, he was fun and funny. "Desperation breeds odd bedfellows" was something my grandmother used to say. I'd never known what it meant until now.

Despite the horrible way I went about it, reminiscing about Nathan, and the crap that went down before I'd come up here, no longer seemed to have the same effect on me it did before going up that mountain trail.

Was it worth almost dying for? The truth was... maybe. At least I was watching two beautiful men dance a beautiful dance of love in an area whose beauty almost hurt the eye. And I didn't feel my heart break every time I thought of Nathan. That was definitely a plus, but I certainly wasn't ready to say all that pain and recovery was worth it.

Joseph returned just before noon with sandwiches and beer in hand. "You all ready for something to eat?" Both Mac and Todd turned, in unison, of course, and waded toward the shore.

"Hey, Daniel," Joseph called. "When we're done eating, would you be able to take a little hike on that trail over there with me? I need to check on a wildlife camera we put up yesterday to see what we caught."

I was hoping to God, the thrill that swept over me didn't show on my face. I replied as calmly as I could, "Sure, I'd like to get a little exercise." From the look on Mac's face, I'm guessing I didn't hide my excitement as well as I'd hoped.

We ate our lunch, as Mac and Todd chatted away about the places they hoped to fish in the park. Joseph patiently answered their questions and occasionally recommended an area off the beaten path for them to visit.

When the guys had returned to their fishing, Joseph led me to the trail he'd mentioned before lunch. It was level and swept alongside the lake.

"You let me know if this is too much and we can walk back," he said over his shoulder.

"Don't worry about me, your dad put me through my paces yesterday and I kept up fine. Seems I'm healing faster than folks thought."

Laughing, Joseph said, "That would be my dad. He sees a set of empty hands, or in your case, one empty hand and he gets a need to fill it up with work."

"I can see that about him, but I honestly didn't mind. In fact, the work was like balm to old wounds."

"Don't feel like you have to help him tomorrow. If he really needs help, I'm off and plan on stopping by his shop anyway. I'll put him off if you prefer."

"Please don't," I said, genuinely concerned I might lose my new job. "I really would enjoy some time around construction stuff for a while. I love your aunt, but if I'm fussed over much more, I think I'll turn into a blob, and she'll mop me up and throw me out the back door."

Joseph chuckled. "No problem, I just didn't want you to feel obligated."

"I don't truly, I really am looking forward to it." I heard the pleading in my voice. I was maybe a bit desperate to have something to do other than lie around Beth's home.

"Well, I have no doubt it'll make the old man happy to have someone willing to be bossed around and I have no problem with that being someone other than me."

I smiled. "So, what is it you are trying to film up here?" I asked.

Joseph turned around and his face lit up as he started to tell me what he was up to.

"We're always surveying the region to see what animals occupy the area and we're particularly interested in seeing how humans affect the animals' movements in the park. This area has pretty significant human use, and we want to see which animals are utilizing this part of the park."

I thought of the snowy owl that'd landed on the bench when I thought I was dying as he talked a bit more about the area and how people could do serious damage to the wildlife as we continued down the path. I almost mentioned the bird, but it felt... wrong somehow. Like the visit from the owl was private and sacred. Something just for me to know.

We arrived at the camera within thirty minutes of leaving the fishing spot. The camera was well hidden, more from people, I guessed, than from the wildlife.

I sat down to enjoy the view, both of the lake, and of Joseph.

Joseph did something with his phone and the camera, then came over to sit down next to me. He thumbed through a few pictures, getting to the ones he'd uploaded from the camera.

"Okay," he said, pointing at a picture, "here are a couple raccoons... several pictures of them, in fact." He chuckled and I could clearly see how much he loved the work. "No surprise, they have very little concern when it comes to humans. Oh, here's a mink. If you look over toward the bank just to our right, you'll see an old log hanging slightly over the side of the lake. That's their den. Mink are shy, but when humans are gone for the night, this is their playground."

Joseph flipped through the photos, almost unaware that I was with him. Suddenly he stopped flipping and said, "Oh, now this is interesting. This is what appears to be a marmot, an Olympic marmot, to be precise." He turned toward me, a light in his eyes that hadn't been there before.

"These are found only in this part of the world." He was so wrapped up in what he was showing me that I don't think he realized just how close he was sitting or how close his face was to mine. Trying not to make something out of nothing, I looked intently at the marmot, which incidentally looked like a cross between a beaver and squirrel. I tried to wait until Joseph moved away.

My God, he smelled like the woods. We were in the woods, and he smelled more like a forest than the forest did. I had to stop it. Maybe I should have faked being in pain so I could stop it before I embarrassed myself, *again*!

Joseph looked over at me.

"Did you know there are several species that live everywhere else in Washington state but here? There are also a few species that only live here... can *only* live here."

Then his expression changed, and with the coolest movement, he leaned the extra few inches between us and kissed me. Just as soon as it started, it ended, leaving me a little lost. When he pulled away, he smiled.

"Maybe we should get back," he said. No explanation, no comment, like nothing even happened.

"Wh... what?" I asked.

Joseph reached down and pulled me up by my good arm. "We don't want the guys to think we've abandoned them, do we?"

"No,"—*fucking fuck, fuck, fuck*, I thought internally—"I guess not."

What did I do wrong? Did my breath smell? Did I smell? Why did he make a move, shock the shit out of me, then pull away? If I wasn't embarrassed before, then I sure as hell was after that.

I didn't say much on the way back down the trail. Mostly I kept my head down and hoped that whatever had put him off wouldn't come up in front of Mac and Todd. I knew it was childish, but I didn't want to have to endure a group of guys, guys I liked and had connected with, making fun of me. I didn't think I could handle that kind of rejection after such an awesome day.

Joseph didn't mention the kiss debacle to Mac and Todd, and the rest of the afternoon was uneventful. Mac offered to help me practice fly fishing with him, but with only one arm, I told him I was likely not going to be very good at it.

He laughed and explained that the key was to learn to pop the fly, and I only needed one hand and arm to do that. I let him show me some of his techniques but the only thing I learned from the exercise was how difficult fly fishing really was.

Growing up, my kind of fishing was cutting a branch off a tree, and tying on a line with a hook and worm on the end. We thought having a weight that wasn't a screw or nut or, even more unlikely, a bobber, was fancy. All three guys found that funny, but Todd said his dad told stories of fishing that way as a kid too.

"Well, I'm a little backwoodsy, I guess," I said.

On the drive home, Mac and Todd wanted to stop at the local grocery store to pick up some wine. Beth had told us before we left that morning that Martha, Joseph's other aunt, was coming over for dinner.

Six

WE ARRIVED TO A house full of commotion and excitement. Martha was a rather short and slender woman with a very sensible haircut that screamed, 'I'm a woman who likes to be in charge.' Kaden was also there and with him was a petite woman with blond hair and a bubbly personality. I instantly liked her, probably because she had an unmistakable glint of mischief that occasionally sparkled in her eyes.

After we'd been introduced to Martha, Beth turned and said, "Kaden, why don't you introduce us all to your *friend*."

"Don't mind if I do. Everyone, this is my friend, Sam Jeffs. She works down at the hospital."

Sam smiled brightly at the introduction. "It is my pleasure to meet all of you." Then looking pointedly at Beth, then at Kaden, she added, "And I hope to be seeing a lot more of you in the future."

Kaden squirmed a bit at her statement, but Beth and Martha beamed. Seemed like Kaden had gotten ahold of a live wire.

The house was full of all kinds of food, enough even to make my Southern women folk pleased. By the time we'd finished eating, I was so full I could have easily just gone to bed. Mac and Todd opened the wine and we all sat around the living room, each of us with protruding bellies.

"So," Martha said smiling. "I hear you have another novel out, Beth. When do you think we'll be able to read it?"

"The publisher hasn't given me a date yet, but if past experience is any indication, I'd say we'll be seeing it hit the shelves by next summer."

I perked up and asked, "Mrs. Beth, you're a writer?

"That's one way to put it," Joseph blurted out.

"Joseph Kaden McCoy, don't make me come over there and help you remember respect!" Martha exclaimed. "The writing your aunt Beth does isn't meant for men; it's meant to help women *deal* with their men."

Joseph seemed to really be enjoying himself.

"You know I love you like my own child, Joseph," Beth chimed in, "but you will never understand the needs of a woman. Good thing you're gay."

She turned back toward me and said, "Daniel, I'm a romance writer."

"Oh," I said, not wanting to create any more strife among the family.

Martha added, "Have you ever heard of the name Annabeth Clemens?"

"No, ma'am, but I'm sure my mom would have known you. She was an avid reader of the romance kind."

"Well, of course, she was," Martha put in. "Most women are. Men have a flawed design when it comes to women. We have needs that men don't seem to ever understand… the need to be swept off our feet, treated like a queen but respected as an equal. Books like Beth's meet those needs even if only vicariously through her characters and allow the women to stay with their men even when they lack those special skills."

Kaden grinned at Martha and said, "I know you've had your share of bad experiences when it comes to men, but not all of us are lacking in the romantic skills."

"Oh, is that so?" Martha bantered. "Then why has everyone you dated been such huge supporters of Beth's writing?"

Kaden was clearly enjoying getting his sister's dander up and continued, "Because, every woman who is well taken care of likes to know her sisters have found someone who's as fulfilled as she is."

"Martha, Kaden," Beth jumped in, "this is a debate you can have later, and since you've been having it since I first got published, I'm sure you will. For now, let's move on to a different topic. Todd, Joseph said you're an attorney down in Seattle. What kind of law do you practice?"

Todd was clearly disappointed the show had ended.

"Oh, this and that. Mostly I work in civil law cases, but occasionally, I get pulled over into misdemeanors and small criminal proceedings. Nothing that exciting, unfortunately," he said.

"And Mac, Joseph said you worked for the county?" Beth continued with the questions.

"I do. I work as a probation officer. That's how we met, actually."

Martha beamed. "Do tell us that story."

Todd and Mac looked at one another and seemed to non-verbally decide who would have the chance to tell everyone how they met. Todd chuckled before launching into the story of how the two had met over a client and how ultimately, they'd become friends before becoming lovers.

Beth looked over at Todd, and with a solemn look, said, "I've written many love stories where the man and woman swirl into a whirlwind romance, but my own love with William simmered low and slow. There were bursts of heat that flamed from time to time, but like you, there was an underlying friendship that seemed to permeate the relationship. I love a hot steamy story, but if you can marry your best friend, you'll always have that no matter what happens with the romance."

"So, how did you boys meet Joseph?" Martha asked.

Mac interjected at that point. "My job is a bit hectic, and sometimes you just have to escape to keep from going off the deep end, so I took a flyfishing class up here several years ago. Joseph was one of the rangers manning the station. He and I hit it off, and he agreed to take me around to some of the different streams to practice. That's when my passion for fly fishing began. Joseph became a friend I kept in contact with, and now whenever we get a chance to get away, we call Joseph and beg him to be our guide."

"If anyone knows the park and the best hidden fishing sites, that would be Joseph. That boy was made for the forest. I'd say it was our native roots but, truth is, neither me nor my siblings have any more desire to be in the woods than any other city folks," Kaden said with a hint of pride in his voice.

Martha looked at her brother. "I don't know, Kaden, you have a way with wood. You can turn a plain old stump into something beautiful. That's a skill that probably passed down through our ancestry."

"I guess you're right," he said. "But we all still have to acknowledge that Joseph is the woodsiest of us or any of our predecessors, at least in recent years."

Kaden looked over at us and added, "Our dad was a politician, and our mother stayed at home with us, but neither seemed to have any interest in the outdoors. Our grandparents, from Dad's side, were first-generation off the reservation, and they focused their efforts on running a small grocery store north of Seattle. Of course, that was before the area was as populated as it is now. Our mom's parents were from someplace out East. We didn't know them well. They didn't really approve of our father."

"Times have certainly changed," Beth added. "My grandparents liked William well enough in the sixties, but there were definitely some not so nice glares from people around here when we first moved back. That being said, it didn't take long before William wormed his way into the hearts of the townsfolk. In the end, I'm sure they liked him much more than they did me. Of course, nowadays, everyone seems to be claiming native roots. So, there's much less of an issue with interracial marriage."

"No, today, the issue on the table is gay marriage," Joseph chimed in, "and whether or not we should have the right to live like every other human on the planet. Even after the Supreme Court ruling, it still seems to be front and center. I guess because we come from native roots, it all just feels like the same story being told again but this time with different characters."

The conversation bounced from person to person throughout the evening. A little past nine, Kaden announced he was going to get Sam back home.

"I'll see you tomorrow, Daniel, if you're still up for it?" he asked as they got ready to leave.

"Looking forward to it," I said. Again, I felt a bit concerned that he might not want me to come out and help again.

The rest of the group dispersed slowly. Mac and Todd said their goodbyes. They decided to back to Edmonds to be ready for work the next day. After spending so much time with Nathan, it was truly refreshing to spend time with a couple of guys that just enjoyed hanging out together with no ulterior motives or any need to outshine anyone else.

I decided that when I got back to Seattle, I was definitely going to look those two up and set up a time to hang out.

Seven

T HE FOLLOWING MORNING, KADEN was at the house at exactly eight. We drove to his workshop in the next town over, without much discussion. When we arrived, there was already coffee ready to go because, thankfully, he'd already put a pot on.

I was looking forward to the work, but I wasn't particularly excited about working without caffeine in my system. I made a straight line for the coffee, and Kaden asked me to pour him a cup as well. We sat for a moment over our coffee while Kaden explained what he wanted me to do while I was there.

My first responsibility was to answer the phone and to keep everyone *the hell away from him*. I was told to take messages but that unless someone was dying, I was to let him handle them when he was done working.

"If I answered that damned phone every time someone needed something, I'd never get a damned thing done," he said.

My second duty was to be there when Kaden needed an extra hand. For the most part, that was just the occasional holding a board, grabbing nails or fetching a tool. The last part of my job was to sweep up as best I could between cuttings.

"No man in his right mind wants to walk all day on a pile of sawdust."

That was exactly how the morning went. Kaden had not exaggerated about the telephone. It rang constantly. Between phone calls, I tried to sweep the sawdust into a pile since I only had one hand and couldn't manage both a broom and a dustpan.

Kaden said he'd get it all swept up at the end of the day if I could just keep it out from underfoot. I was only asked to help grab a tool or hold a board once or twice, and mostly, I thought Kaden just wanted to check up on me when he asked.

Around noon, Kaden stopped, stretched his back, went over to the fridge, and pulled out some of last night's leftovers.

We were just finishing up when Joseph arrived. I didn't mean to be cold, but I'd forgotten he was coming, and I didn't want him to tell his father whatever it was that had put him off me. On top of that, I didn't want a repeat experience either. I didn't know what was going on with him but, beautiful or not, but I was in no mood for more games.

Kaden had a list of chores for Joseph to complete, so we didn't really have time to talk about embarrassing situations. Joseph brought up the subject of *Space Needle Rehab* show and asked whether his aunt was inundating me with it.

Both Kaden and he laughed when I confirmed she watched the show a lot. "I think she might have a bit of a crush on Les Cooper," I said.

"No doubt," Kaden said. "But in her defense, he does have the same build as my late brother did. She definitely has a type."

I chuckled at the thought. "Well, it's a cool show. It's fun to watch those old homes turned back into beauties."

"Yeah," Kaden said shaking his head. "Shame their last home got destroyed, they'd done a great job with it."

Around four o'clock, Kaden said it was time to be done for the day since he needed to run a couple errands. I turned to get my things, but just as I did, I heard Joseph volunteer to take me back to Beth's place. Hell, how was I supposed to get out of that? Not being able to think of a way out, I decided to just roll with the punches. The ride to Beth's was pretty short, so there wasn't going to be much time for discussion. Kaden agreed and asked if I'd be willing to come back for another day tomorrow.

"I'm free the rest of the week if you can use me," I told him.

"I can definitely use you every day, except for Thursday. Umm... I have plans that day."

Joseph waggled his eyebrows at his dad and immediately got a nasty look from him.

Laughing, Joseph turned toward me and said, "If you're ready, let's head out."

When we got into the car, Joseph leaned over and tried to kiss me again.

"What the hell are you doing?" I stopped him. "Listen, Joseph, I don't know what games you're playing but I'm not interested. If you don't mind, I'm really tired and could use some more painkillers. Do you mind driving me back to Beth's?"

The usual half-smile that seemed to linger on Joseph's face faded. "I didn't mean to upset you. I thought you liked me. That's the message I got from you yesterday, at least."

"Like you? I'm probably going to regret this but let me be real straight with you. I did like you... do like you, but you have to understand, I came up here, hiked up a mountain trail I was in no shape to climb, and ended up having to be carried off the mountain on a stretcher because I let the games of a so-called friend get the better of me. If it's games you're into, then I am not your guy."

Joseph truly looked perplexed. "I'm not sure where you got the idea that I was a player, but you can ask anyone who knows me, I shoot straight. What did I do to make you so upset?"

"Well, you kissed me, then walked away like I had serious B.O. or something."

"Oh," he said frowning, "I see..."

"Seriously, Joseph, I'm really beginning to hurt here. I enjoyed the work at your dad's, and I think I overdid it a little. Maybe I'm a little jumpy and most definitely not in the right frame of mind to understand your advances, so if you don't mind, I'd really like to get some painkillers in me."

Joseph looked defeated, and I felt like a total ass, but the pain in my arm had transitioned from a low thrumming to full-out torture, and on top of that, I was beginning to get a headache. I laid my head back and took a little nap as we drove back to Beth's.

Interestingly, that was the first time since I'd met Joseph that I wasn't embarrassed but was full-out pissed at him. Somehow, he'd led me on, kissed me, and then left me feeling like a cad. Now I was supposed to feel sorry for him? No, buddy, you do not get to be the victim in this story.

Finally, we arrived at Beth's. I darted back to my room, popped the medication and laid down until the pain in both my head and my arm subsided. I didn't need the drama of another man in my life. I didn't need drama at all right now. I was scheduled to be in court next week to deal with the drama from the last event involving a man.

I resolved then and there that there would be no more kissing the handsome Joseph. *Your looks are not going to influence me now.* The only thing I wanted that week was to rest, recover, and play with some power tools. Then I was going to go home, face the music, possibly get to know a new cellmate, probably named Bubba, and that would be that.

I fell asleep shortly after taking my pills and woke up to a darkened world. How long had I slept? I got up to look at the clock to see that it was shortly after ten. Oh shit, maybe I really had overdone it at Kaden's workshop.

With consciousness came a deep and real hunger. I slipped out of my room and into the kitchen, hoping not to disturb anyone, but also hoping to snag some leftovers from last night's feast.

Beth saw me from the living room. "Honey, did you sleep well?" she asked.

"I did, thanks. But unfortunately, I woke up hungry enough to eat a horse."

"Good, that's a good sign. Look over there in the microwave. I saved you some food from dinner."

If I hadn't already fallen in love with Beth, the sight of a full meal wrapped in plastic wrap would have sealed the deal, and I told her as much as I waited for the food to heat up.

"You overdid it with Kaden today, and I've already put him in his place about it."

"Oh no, Mrs. Beth, it wasn't anything Mr. Kaden did or didn't do. I overdid it because I was having a good time. I've never seen anyone with the woodworking skills he has. It's like watching a sculptor build a masterpiece."

"Well, you're correct there at least, but you were put in my care to help you heal, and I'm not about to stand by and watch you turn back the clock. Maybe you should stay here tomorrow. Kaden has already agreed."

"No, I don't think I could stand another day in the sickbed. I'll make a deal with you, I'll take my meds with me, and if I start feeling fatigued, I'll pull back and rest until I feel better. Deal?"

Reluctantly, Beth agreed. "Kaden said he doubted I'd be able to talk you into staying here tomorrow. In fact, I may end up owing him a wager, but never mind all that. If you start to feel fatigued in any way, I will come get you myself." We nodded at each other in agreement.

As I ate my salvation dinner, I decided to get to the bottom of a few questions about who had put me in her care to begin with.

"Mrs. Beth, I was so out of it when I came here that I have no idea how the whole thing came about. How did you end up with me here in the first place? I know it wasn't my brother because I didn't tell him I was this bad until after I was already here. Was it the hospital or the rangers?"

"I probably shouldn't let all the cats out of this bag, but I will say this, you've had a knight in shining armor since he found you on that mountain."

"Ranger Mike?" I asked, confused.

Beth looked at me seriously. "I know you aren't dense. Who do you remember seeing on that mountain that has consistently seen you since?"

"Joseph," I sighed.

"Yes, Joseph. You made some kind of impression on that kid, and I'll tell you something, not many people do make a good impression with Joseph. Until you came around, I've never seen him make any attempt at getting to know another man, at least not in an *interested* sort of way. I think that's why we've all been so curious about you."

"So, Joseph was the one to set all this up. Did he also gather up all my gear and get my car here?"

She smiled in acknowledgment. "Had it not been for Joseph, the park rangers would have just bundled you back down to Seattle. It also seems you have a past, and that past was certainly not something that was motivating the rangers into helping you more than necessary."

"Oh," I sighed. "Well, that's a long story and one I'm happy to share with you, but first, I need to confess that on the drive back home, I might have deflated any balloons Joseph might have had."

Beth looked on but didn't offer that she knew more than what I was telling her. "After leaving Kaden's, Joseph tried to kiss me... *again.*"

"Again?" Beth asked, and cocked an eyebrow in surprise.

"Yeah, the first time was yesterday, but he kissed me, then pulled me up off my ass and walked away. I figured that he decided he wasn't interested or that I had cooties or something. So, when he leaned over to kiss me this afternoon, the frustration from yesterday mixed with throbbing pain in my arm and an oncoming headache made me overreact a bit. I might have told him to shove his interest and not in a nice way."

I waited for Beth to chastise me, but instead, she let out a huge laugh. "Oh, well done, my boy, well done. I won't give away my nephew's tactics, but he kind of sees love as a battle, and he may have thought you were a player. Even though this is mutiny, I'll tell you he probably thought the only way to win your love was to outplay you."

"So, that explains a lot. He knows I punched a guy, but doesn't know why... but he assumes it's because I'm a player. He probably also thinks I'm an arrogant city slicker who doesn't know my own boundaries, which is why I was caught falling off a damned mountain and needing to be rescued like a simple-minded damsel in distress."

"Now, before you get too carried away here, let me remind you of two things. One, Joseph doesn't put much effort into 'saving damsels in distress' and two, you did fall off a mountain, and you did punch a guy in the face and were arrested for it from what I hear."

Deflated, I decided Beth deserved the whole story, so before I pounced on her nephew any further, I explained all the sordid details between Nathan, Tony and myself. I also told her I was so upset by Nathan's betrayal that I came up here to get away. I'd climbed the trail because I needed some physical activity that drove the never-ending thoughts of those two out of my head.

"So, Mrs. Beth, you see, I'm not an arrogant city slicker, and I'm not a player. When Joseph kissed me and then left me hanging, I assumed he was playing his own form of my ex-friend Nathan's game, and I just couldn't handle it."

Beth looked me over for a moment, then let the smile return to her face. "Lovers are always the same, straight or gay. You always let the past cloud your future. Both you and Joseph are equally guilty of miscommunication, and the truth is you both have reasons not to trust, but let me give you just a little advice. If you are truly looking for a loyal man, one who would turn the world upside down for the one he loved, you will never find one as loyal as Joseph."

"Now that I've officially crossed fully over onto the enemy's side," she said while wiping down the front of her blouse, "I'll leave this conversation with just one more statement. I know my nephew as well as any other human on the planet does since William, and I love him like the kid we never had.

"If you want a chance to make things right with Joseph, you better make that happen soon because once he heads back into those woods, he will be like a dog licking his wounds. None of us will see him again until he is done and over you. Sounds harsh, but that is the way of him."

Beth got up then and headed back to her bedroom but not before stopping and patting my shoulder. "Just think about what I said."

After the conversation, I found myself weary again and went back to bed, fearing that I wouldn't be able to sleep. But after a few moments thinking about how badly Joseph and I had botched the whole thing, I ended up falling asleep hard and fast.

I stood on the cliff overlooking the water outside the back of Beth's home. I looked up just as the snowy owl flew over my head and out across the sea. It flew only a few moments before I saw it hovering over the water as if it were waiting for something.

I was shocked when a large body lifted up out of the water. Even from this distance I could tell it belonged to a large orca whale. The owl hovered over the whale for a long time, appearing as if they were somehow communicating with one another.

Eventually, the whale submerged again, and the owl turned back toward me.

I could see the owl was picking up speed, and when it came upon me, just as if it were about to attack its prey, it stuck its talons out. Before it reached me, I woke up, sweat beads running down my face.

Eight

I COULD HEAR VOICES in the kitchen, so I crawled out of bed, went to the bathroom, and splashed some water on my face to get the strange dream out of my head before I came back to the room to get dressed. I found Joseph and Kaden standing at Beth's kitchen island. Kaden looked over and said, "The dead have arisen."

"Yeah, the dead is right," I replied miserably. "I forgot to turn my alarm on. If you can give me a moment, I can be changed and ready to go."

"No need to hurry, I have an errand to run, and Joseph has agreed to bring you over to the shop once you've gotten ready."

Beth looked at me pointedly and said, "Now that is a solid plan, brother-in-law, a very solid plan."

I looked over at Joseph and asked, "Do I have time for a quick shower? I was too out of it to grab one last night and I'm afraid if I don't get one now, I'm liable to drive you both from the workshop."

Kaden smiled and teased me. "Don't want no smelly dudes chasing off all the pretty women at my shop."

"That's truer than you might think. Don't look so confused, Daniel," Beth retorted. "How many of the phone calls you took yesterday were from women? Since moving up to Port Angeles, single women from miles around seem to have a multitude of odd jobs for our Kaden to do."

"I agree, the majority of my clientele in Port Angeles are women, but the same was true when I was building furniture in Seattle, sis-in-law. I think I get the calls because I'm quick and good with a hammer," Kaden responded.

"That and you're single," Beth said as she walked toward the living room.

I learned that the siblings, as I've come to think of Kaden, his sister Martha, and their sister-in-law Beth, were as close as they could be. I'd come to love the banter between them and secretly wished my brother and I were as close. Maybe after our talk, things would change for the better, but I could never imagine that level of closeness and camaraderie ever happening between Paul and myself.

I grabbed a shower as fast as my injured arm would let me and was ready in less than twenty minutes. I came back out, and both Kaden and Beth had gone.

Joseph sat on a stool at the kitchen island, drinking a cup of coffee and looking out over the view from Beth's kitchen window. When I came in, he looked over and smiled. "Before we go, can I talk to you for a few minutes?"

"Yeah," I said, and a blush rose on my cheeks. "I wanted to talk to you as well. Me first, okay?" Joseph nodded for me to go ahead. "I really apologize for jumping on you last night. I was beginning to feel some pain from my arm... but that isn't really why. I am very attracted to you, and I think that's been clear since the first time I laid eyes on you, but something bad happened to me before I came up here. In fact, that's *why* I came up here."

"Daniel," Joseph cut in. "It isn't my business what brought you here. I was out of line kissing you without checking in with you, and I understand why you'd think I was playing games. In a way, I guess I was."

"No," I shook my head. "I want to clear the air, and because you're behind my rescue, in a lot more ways than just taking me off the mountain, I feel like you have a right to know. Besides, if this is going to go anywhere, I need things to be... clear."

Joseph sat back then and let me talk.

"As I was saying, something bad happened to me in Seattle, and I already know that you are aware of some of it, but knowing I was arrested doesn't tell you the whole story. I have... *had* a friend that I was or at least thought I was close to. We weren't lovers, mind you, but I thought we were friends. Nathan, that's his name, was really the first guy friend I've ever had that I thought was the real deal. I used to work as a bartender at one of the gay bars downtown. One night I came into work and when I walked in, Nathan was standing in the corner. I could tell he was kissing another guy, but I couldn't see who it was until I came up to the counter. Nathan stepped away for a moment, and I saw that the guy he was playing tongue hockey with was my boyfriend, Tony.

"Something snapped inside me. One minute I'm standing next to the bar, the next, my fist was in Nathan's face." I chuckled a bit at that point. "I have really never hit anyone before. Truth is, I've never been in a fight. It seemed like someone else took ahold of me, and next thing I know, Nathan's nose was bloody."

When Joseph continued to watch me, I went on with my story. "My boss came out of the back just in time to see me clobber Nathan and yelled, that I was fired and worthless and needed to get out. Just like that, I lost my friend, my boyfriend, and my job, all in one inconceivable moment."

I crashed down on the chair and rubbed my forehead before continuing. "When I got home, a police officer was standing at my door. To add insult to injury, Officer Sparks is a friend of my brother and his husband. So, on top of losing my job and my friends, I also got to add humiliation to the list."

I looked Joseph in the eye before continuing. "When my brother-in-law bailed me out, I came up here to get away from the whole situation, knowing that if I stayed, Nathan would make sure things got worse between us. As far as how I met you goes, I climbed that trail because I wanted some extreme exercise to wear myself out and hopefully stop thinking about my predicament and to stop feeling sorry for myself. I fell down the mountain because I wasn't paying attention. So, when you and the others had to rescue me, it was just another stupid thing

I'd done in a string of stupid things, and I was nothing if not mortified by the whole experience."

Joseph reached over and placed a hand over mine.

"Daniel, I don't know many men who wouldn't have clobbered the son of a bitch for having his tongue down your boyfriend's throat. That doesn't shock or concern me. As a ranger, I most certainly can't say it's okay that you weren't paying attention, especially on a mountain hike as dangerous as Pyramid. However, all the guys, including me, were very impressed at how you handled yourself in a dangerous situation. We had a hiker fall to his death there last spring, and had to airlift a couple hikers last year from the very place you fell. Due to the severity of your injury, it surprised all of us that you were able to get yourself to a safe elevation and put yourself where hikers would find you the following day. So, there is no need for you to be embarrassed. Just, from now on, make sure someone knows where you are when you go hike a dangerous trail. Had you done that, you wouldn't have had to spend the night in pain and in the cold."

Joseph waited until I looked up from playing with my cuticles before continuing, "You are the first guy I've had these kinds of feelings for in... in a very long time. Most of my days are spent surveying animals, making reports on what I find, and helping out the occasional injured park visitor. I live a pretty secluded life and that's by choice, so when I felt that attraction toward you, I was as shocked as I could tell you were."

Joseph took a deep breath and let it out slowly while using his right hand to smooth back his hair. "I have my own apologies to make as well, and one of those was assuming you were something you're not. I'll be honest, I decided while we were hauling you down off the trail that, come hell or high water, I was going to get to know the real you." Joseph took a sip of his coffee and looked back out the window.

"Like you, I've had some pretty rough experiences and the guys I tried dating in the past all turned out to be self-centered players. You deserve the chance to be who you are without me putting all that on you."

He looked down sheepishly then. "When I kissed you by the lake, I was testing the boundaries, just checking to see if you felt the same way I did. When you responded, I decided to let you squirm a bit while keeping myself in control. Then when I tried to kiss you yesterday, I had clearly not checked to see where and how you were before doing so. That makes me an ass, and I'm sorry... very sorry for that. If you'd be willing to give me another chance, I promise to make it up to you. I'll be the perfect gentleman and only kiss you if, and when, you want me to."

Smiling, I leaned over toward him. "I'd kinda like for you to kiss me right now."

Joseph smiled back and right before kissing me said, "I was hoping you'd say that."

Kissing Joseph felt as if the planets had finally aligned. Unfortunately, when he pulled back, he frowned saying he would've loved to spend the evening with me, but that he had to put some hours in at the ranger station, and tonight he was on-call with the rescue squad.

"However," he added quickly, "if you're up to it Thursday, I have a standing invitation to go sailing with a buddy of mine. You can get a totally different view of the park from the water than you can on land."

I was excited by the thought but also concerned. "You know I only have one hand, so I'm not going to be much help hoisting sails."

Joseph laughed. "Most of the time, my friend Peter sails alone, so unless there's rough water, Peter and I can handle things without you doing much."

Truth be told, I loved being out on the water, and besides the occasional ferry ride across the Sound, I rarely got the chance.

After thinking for a couple of moments, I said, "Yes, I'd love to, but make sure there's enough time for more kissing," and winked at him.

Joseph laughed heartily and kissed me again, this time pulling me up and into his incredibly hot self. When he let me go, all I could think of was being wrapped up in his delightfully muscular arms and pressed against that hard, long body of his.

Once he'd dropped me off at his dad's workshop and left, I sat on the chair in the office and rehashed the events that had unfolded. "Damn, what a morning," I said aloud. I need to make sure I do something really special for Beth. Had it not been for our talk last night, well, and maybe the strange dream,

I would likely not have given Joseph the chance to clear things up. That would have sucked because I really looked forward to kissing Joseph again in the future! Hell, I didn't know if I'd think about anything else between now and then.

I couldn't have been more wrong. Answering the phone at Kaden's was never-ending, and the calls that came in were twice as many as the day before. Kaden told me I should warn everyone that he wouldn't be able to do any work for them for at least three months.

I took messages and tried to help sweep when I got the chance. By the time Kaden dropped me off at Beth's house, I was worn out.

Nine

THE FOLLOWING MORNING, KADEN picked me up saying he had a surprise.

"But you have to promise me you won't go around telling people who we are meeting today," he said.

Kaden didn't strike me as someone to play games or keep secrets so I knew this must be pretty important for him to ask.

"Sure, who would I tell anyway? Joseph or Beth?" I asked.

He smiled and said, "Well, they already know, but you can't tell your brother. I probably shouldn't even be taking you with me, but I thought you could use a change in scenery, and I wanted some company on the drive."

We chatted about his business and all it entailed as we drove the two-and-a-half hours from Port Angeles to Seattle. Of course, being typical Pacific Northwesterners, we stopped for coffee twice on the way.

By the time we pulled up in front of the huge mansion that sat on Lake Washington, Kaden and I had already begun to get closer. I really did like the man. He seemed to like me too. I knew without a shadow of a doubt, had my father been alive, he and Kaden would've been best buddies. The thought of that warmed my heart.

We got out of the car and I instantly heard the sounds of construction. I figured the old mansion must be some kind of renovation project, with all the construction vehicles sitting in the yard, and the sounds just confirmed it.

We were stopped before we could go into the house by a couple of armed guards. That did shock me.

Kaden showed them a letter and the woman ended up taking it before disappearing into the house. She came back out a moment later with Les Cooper in her wake.

"No fucking way," I said under my breath. Kaden chuckled, then elbowed me in the side while saying, "Hush."

I did as instructed. Les Cooper, the big Home Repair Network star. Beth had forced me to watch almost every episode the man starred in, and now he was for real standing right in front of me. I knew he was in Seattle working on projects, but I wouldn't have ever thought I'd meet him. I immediately looked around to see if Bennett Jackson was also here, but I didn't see him.

Les smiled as he walked off the porch and shook hands with Kaden. "I can't tell you how excited my mom will be that you agreed to take this on," he said.

"She did sort of twist my arm," Kaden replied with a chuckle.

"Oh man, I know how that goes. She's my mom after all."

Les acknowledged me then, and I followed the two men into the house to meet Les's family. They were all spread around the big home doing various projects. When a camera moved toward us, Les put his hand up.

"Sorry, Mr. McCoy specifically said he wouldn't allow any filming of him or his work until it was done and installed," he told the cameraman.

I could tell the cameraman was disappointed. I would be too; Kaden was a hunk even if he was twice my age. I'm sure the camera would've love him.

I was speechless when Les asked if I would be willing to be filmed.

"Um, no... I'm just a grunt worker," I said, putting my good hand out in a stop motion.

Both Kaden and Les chuckled. "I sort of threw the boy into this."

I gave Kaden the eye, but I'm sure my smile betrayed my effort to look upset.

I got to meet Les's family and learn how hard they'd had to pursue Kaden to get him to build the custom cabinets and various other woodworking items for this huge house.

I liked them all. I mean, I really liked them. Even though I could see them filming different segments for the show, there was no major pretense going on. Mostly, just a group of professionals getting their work done.

I didn't get to meet Bennett that day, but I honestly didn't think I would. He'd been put through the wringer, so to speak, with his father and other issues. I was sure he was still somewhere recovering. I didn't ask either. If all the rumors were true,

I'm sure everyone would be sensitive and protective of him. I know I would've been.

I helped Kaden take measurements for the kitchen cabinets and then followed him and Les's mother around as she showed him where she wanted him to build some other things for the property.

I could see it all in my mind and it was going to be spectacular. I desperately wanted to be a part of the project, but I knew I couldn't. I'd be back in Seattle long before they even got started, but that didn't mean I couldn't wish for it.

On the way back to Port Angeles, I didn't realize I was sitting quietly until Kaden reached over and nudged me.

"Did I overwhelm you back there?" he asked in good humor.

"You did, I mean, thank you though. I knew Les and his family had taken over the Home Repair Network show in Seattle, but I would've never thought I'd get to meet them."

"They're just people, and good people from what I can tell, but yeah, it's fun to meet someone you see on television."

"So, do Joseph and Beth know you're going to build their custom cabinets? I mean that's sort of a huge honor, isn't it?"

Kaden just laughed. "They know, but son, I've been making cabinets and built-ins longer than you've been alive. I don't do it for show any longer, I just do it because I still love doing it. It is an honor they want me to do the work, but it's an honor when anyone appreciates what I do and wants me to do it for them."

I nodded. "I think I'd feel the same..."

Kaden regarded me a moment before turning his attention back to the road. I was still in a happy bliss when we got back to his workshop. Of course, there's no rest for the wicked and the moment we got back, Kaden went to his computer to put in the measurements, and he sat me down at the desk to check all the messages, of which there were twenty-seven.

I must admit I was a little starstruck. Not so much of Les, who of course was a handsome television hunk but anyone with a brain knew he only had the hots for Bennett. No, I was enamored by the cabinetmaker who was good enough to work for them. I was struck by Kaden McCoy.

Ten

Luckily, I was able to sleep in on Thursday, and Joseph didn't pick me up until after ten. I warned him that I might need to crash at some point during the day due to the fatigue that still plagued me and my arm. He assured me he'd already taken that into consideration. I was beginning to realize that Beth had been spot-on when it came to Joseph's attention to detail.

I wondered for just a moment how Nathan would have behaved had I been injured and not able to go a full day without resting or taking medication. He'd have been a jerk about it, no doubt, and avoided me until I was healed. I knew I was comparing apples and rotten oranges, but the difference between the two men was striking.

Peter, Joseph's friend, ended up being an old hippie who looked like he was born on the sea. I quickly discovered the best way to help with sailing was to stay out of his way. We skirted the western tip of the Peninsula while Joseph pointed out different wildlife on the shore and in the water. We saw sea turtles, sharks, and a variety of other creatures. Joseph seemed to be on fire as he pointed and described what we saw. From time to time, he'd pull his notebook out and jot down the animals he saw and their GPS location.

"We used to use latitude and longitude, but nowadays it's easier just to use the GPS coordinates," he explained when I asked what he was writing. "It's important to keep notes on the wildlife along the coast just as it is in the forests. We've really done a number on the wildlife population in America, and this area is particularly at risk due to increased population and tourism."

The day was gorgeous, not too hot, not too cold. All you needed was a light jacket. There was a gentle breeze that kept the sails tight, and Peter said we were lucky because he didn't need to use the engine once. We kept tight along the shore until mid-afternoon, at which point Peter told Joseph, "I'm going to do something a little different since you have your friend with you today. I'm going to head out away from shore. Daniel, have you ever seen a whale?"

"No," I responded. "The closest I've come is seeing an orca breaching several miles away from shore while I was camping on the Oregon Coast."

Peter smiled. "Today may just be your lucky day. There's a resident pod of orca here that I'm willing to bet we'll run across. The salmon run seems to be pretty healthy this year, and they're pretty full and happy. But, if you are really lucky, you'll get a look at some of the gray whales that are passing through these parts. I can't promise anything, but yesterday I ran across several pods. If my past experiences are any indicator, they will still be coming through today."

Unable to contain my excitement, I burst out, "Peter, I've always wanted to go whale watching. I'd about give my eyetooth to see one."

That delighted both Peter and Joseph, and they set out for the deeper waters offshore. We sailed on for what seemed about an hour before we spotted dolphins, orca, and other sea life but no gray whales.

Peter sighed and said, "I told you there was no guarantee, but I'm just a bit surprised we haven't run across any. Orca could have scared them off."

I was resigned, but I didn't want to show any disappointment after such an incredible day. I walked over and sat toward the back of the boat. Stern, I think they call it. Joseph came over and sat next to me, asking if I was okay.

I threw my head back, letting the cool breeze and sea spray roll across me.

"I'm more than okay. I'm happier than I think I've ever been. This place is beautiful, full of life, and you and Peter make the whole thing feel like I'm watching National Geographic, which incidentally is one of my favorite channels."

"So," he added, "not disappointed about missing the whales?"

"Oh," I said, "maybe I'm a little sad the whales didn't make an appearance, but no, I am not disappointed."

Joseph smiled that beautiful smile of his and leaned over and kissed me gently on the lips. I moaned happily.

"What was that for?" I asked, thrilled by the feeling of his lips once again on mine.

"Because," he replied, "I can see today made you happy, and knowing that makes me happy. So, I just couldn't help but kiss your adorable, happy face."

"In that case, two can play at that game and the hell with PDA. Peter," I yelled over toward the older man. "Look the other way." Just as I leaned into kiss Joseph, a huge whale leaped out of the water less than a hundred feet from the boat. I sucked in a breath and screamed in both surprise and delight.

"Seems like you got yourself a humpback, young man!" Peter exclaimed. "Don't see many of them this time of year."

"Can I see more of him?" I asked as I rushed over to the side of the boat where the whale had just crashed down.

"Just keep watching," he said. "If he's feeding, he'll be coming up for more again very soon."

Just then, he appeared once again, not breaching quite as much as he had before but certainly enough to see him clearly from the side.

"He's enormous! Are you sure he won't accidentally run into us and tip us over? I saw that happen on Facebook."

"No," Peter chuckled. "It's unlikely. He knows where we are, and he doesn't fancy running into us any more than we want to run into him."

"How do you know it's a male?" I asked.

Joseph laughed. "Well, unless he turns over or starts singing, we probably won't know, but most of the females traveling through at this point have a calf with them. This could be a mother who lost a calf but more likely, it's a male."

We watched the whale breach a few more times before Peter started heading back into port. The trip left me refreshed, relaxed, and happier than I knew I could be. We stepped onto the pier, and Joseph helped Peter secure the sailboat.

Peter said he was happy to begin the process of converting a land lover, and I assured him I was an avid participant in that transformation. We parted ways with an invitation to return anytime to go back out.

Once we'd returned to the car, Joseph asked if I had enough left in me to go grab a bite to eat. "I've got more energy than I've had in years, and I'm hungry enough to eat... well, to eat a whale."

Laughing, he said, "I had something a little less fatty in mind. There's a little café just around the corner from here. It's a bit of a dive, but the food is tasty. Do you trust me?"

"Yep," I responded happily, as I found myself tucked back into his arms. "I trust you completely." I was surprised to find that I really did.

The café was indeed a dive, but the service was great and the food a step above the rest. I'm guessing few if any tourists knew about the place, which helped keep it small and friendly.

After eating, Joseph and I walked along the pier. Joseph reached over and put his hand in mine. Being from the South, I immediately looked around to see what dangers came from such PDA. When Joseph noticed my reaction, he laughed and said, "Nothing to worry about here."

"If you say so," I conceded. "But if we get into a fight with a redneck, you're on your own. I'd like to keep the breaks in this arm down to five. Besides, I've retired my gloves, at least until I get through this court appearance."

"I promise this area is friendly. It's unlikely anyone will even notice."

I believed him and allowed myself to just walk along, enjoying the scenery, and being close to a man who did incredible things to my insides.

We talked for hours, first about me and my legal issues, but eventually, the conversation turned to family and how he loved having his close by and how lucky he felt living so close to the park.

He'd hated growing up in the city and would spend the summers up here with his Aunt Beth and Uncle William. When he graduated from college, it was the only place he wanted to be. He was lucky to get a position at the park, even if it was part-time.

"I don't think anyone would love working in the park as much as you do." I told him.

Joseph smiled. "You're right. I love doing this with everything that's in me. I prefer the outdoors to indoors any day, but there's stiff competition for park jobs. I was in the right place at the right time or else I'd never have gotten that position. The grant ends this year, and everyone tells me if I want to get a full-time job with the Park Service, I'll have to go back to school and finish my master's."

I felt sad that Joseph might be forced to leave his beloved park. "Any thought where you'll do your study?"

"I'm not interested in leaving this part of the world, so I'm guessing it'll be the University of Washington back in Seattle. I've taken several graduate courses over the past few years, so my advisors tell me I should be able to complete my master's in just one year."

"I hate you'll have to leave the park, but if you're going to be in Seattle, I'd like to see more of you."

"Looks like that's exactly what's going to happen, like it or not, right?" he said on a shrug.

I cuddled into him as much to comfort him as to feel his body next to mine.

"Joseph, I warn you, I'm going to get a little mushy, so put your big boy pants on for a minute, okay? I really needed a friend and I appreciate more than you will ever realize you taking on that role. When I saw Nathan kissing Tony, I felt like I couldn't have a friend. Like something was wrong with me. You barely know me, and you've done one thing after another to make my life easier. You really did save my life." He held me silently as I let the emotions pass over me. "You know, I'll admit that right now, I need a friend more than I need a lover but that being said, I also really like kissing you."

He smiled. "I like that too. I've got an idea, let's do less big boy pants talking and a lot more kissing. Deal?"

I laughed at how quickly he was able to turn off the emotional chatter. "You got a deal for now, but it is important that you know what all you've done means to me."

Joseph pulled me closer. "I do know, and I appreciate that."

We rolled into the driveway, and he asked me if I wanted him to come in.

"Yes, I really do, but no, I can't. I know it sounds lame, but I need us to be friends for a while before we switch to anything else. Call me crazy, but can you give me a little more time?"

"No problem. I just didn't want you to think I don't want to dance naked with you. Daniel..." his voice grew deeper, and I felt his breath in my ear. "I really want to get naked with you."

My ears were sensitive, and with that whispered promise, need prickled along my skin. A gentle brush of his whiskered chin also set every nerve ending in my body on fire. All my good intentions of being Joseph's friend first before sex went flying out the window.

"Fuck it," I said, and I leaned my whole body into him. Luckily, the car's console, along with my pinned arm, kept me from jumping him. Before I could rip his clothes off, he pulled back.

It did me some good to see that the move had cost him.

"Slow down there, tiger. I agreed to take it slow, but if you move on me like that, there won't be anything slow about what I'll do to you."

"Not the way to cool me off, Joseph," I said on a sigh.

"No, me either, but it's the truth. I want this to last, Daniel, and my instincts tell me you were right by slowing things down. We both need to trust first, fuck later. I promise you with every breath I take, I will fuck you, and it will be something worth waiting for."

To put the moment aside, I switched tactics and went for humor. "How do you know you'll be doing the fucking? I may be a top."

"Oh, I think that can be arranged too, but the first time we make love, I promise it will be me on top. I've fantasized about you and your body since I first saw you. I know it sounds kind of strange, but maybe because you were vulnerable and the fact that you hated it. Not to mention the look you gave me sent a level of need through me I have never felt before. I haven't had a lot of lovers, but I believe our love-making will be something neither of us has experienced before."

To save me from spontaneous combustion, I stepped out of the car and went over to Joseph's window to lean in and kiss him. "I think it's better you stay behind that door, or the promise I'll make right now is that you will not be going home tonight."

"Daniel, I lust you..."

"What?" I laughed nervously.

"I don't know you well enough to love you yet, but I lust you... and I wanted to say something like that."

"I lust you too, Joseph. Now go home and take a cold shower."

"No thanks, I have other plans to handle these feelings," he said wickedly.

"Go home, Joseph," I said, grinding my teeth to get my own libido under control.

He was laughing as he pulled out of the driveway while I waved.

I realized for the first time I wasn't going to get out of this relationship unscathed. Fuck me. I didn't usually go around saying sweet things, even *I lust you,* until I knew someone really well. But I suspected nothing I had with Joseph would be normal.

As fate would have it, I didn't really see much of Joseph until after the weekend. He had drawn the short straw with the rescue squad and had to work. I was able to get a few hours with him Sunday night before he literally passed out on my lap while we were watching a chick flick with Beth. It had taken all my willpower to keep from inviting him to spend the night with me. Instead, Beth and I left him to sleep the night away on her more-than-comfortable overstuffed couch.

Monday morning, I had a doctor's appointment, and I asked Joseph if he'd like to go with me and then grab a bit of lunch afterward.

"Of course," he said. "Any excuse to spend more time with you."

"That was my thought too." I was glad we were thinking alike.

I tried to talk him into waiting in the lobby while I went back because if the doc took off the cast, I knew from experience how unsexy the smell could be.

Joseph reminded me that he spent his entire life looking for and analyzing animal poo, and my cast couldn't smell nearly as bad as bear poo. Never having smelled bear poo, I was in no position to disagree. As I'd suspected, the doctor took off my hard cast and moved me into a soft one with the stern warning to keep it safe and not move it too much.

"You still have healing to do," he said.

If you've never experienced having a cast on your arm for weeks on end and the discomfort and inconvenience of it, then you'll never know how wonderful it was to be relieved of the burden. Even though I still had to wear the soft cast, and my arm was bound to my chest, I was free of the worst.

"Let's go celebrate. My arm hurts like a bitch, and I'd rather medicate it with a beer than another dose of Ibuprofen."

"I know just where to go," Joseph said and winked at me. "Do you mind loud music?"

"Umm, did you miss the part where I was a bartender? I live for loud music."

Joseph laughed and turned the car into an alley that led to a dead end. He got out as I looked around. "I don't see a bar here."

"Nope, not a bar, something better," he said.

We walked up a flight of rickety stairs, and Joseph knocked on a door perched at the top of an equally rickety deck.

"Joseph, I just got my cast off. I don't fancy another one this soon."

Laughing, he clearly enjoyed whatever secret rendezvous he'd concocted, and referring to the deck, said, "It'll hold, trust me."

I was seriously focused on standing on the supports close to the wall, so I didn't see the door open as much as I heard the noise when it did. I turned to see a middle-aged man dressed in tight black clothes that accentuated his very large mid-section. I was so startled by his appearance, I forgot to be afraid of the lack of support for the deck and stepped over to the man's hand as it shot out with a gleeful welcome.

Joseph shouted to be heard over the music. "Daniel, this is Marcus, or Mark for short. Mark, this is Daniel, my new fling."

"Fling?" I asked and was quickly pulled into the dark, noisy room by Mark's friendly hand.

"It is very nice to see our friend Joseph with a fling, boyfriend, or any interest other than the wild beasts he's always chasing around," Mark said.

Joseph leaned over and said, "This is Mark's recording studio. It sounds like they have The Smoky Rags recording at the moment. They are a local band."

"I figured that since I didn't recognize the music."

"Mark, Daniel just got his cast removed and wanted to celebrate with some loud music and beer. I thought you might be the man to satisfy both needs."

Mark smiled. "You've come to the right place. What kind of beer do you like, domestic or foreign?"

"My favorite is Red Stripe." I smiled.

"We happen to have one left. For you, Joseph?"

"I'll have a Bud if you've got any left."

"Coming right up." Mark left the room.

"How do you know Mark?" I asked.

He's one of Dad's friends from when they were kids. Dad would come up to visit William and Beth when he was a teenager. Mark and him would get into all kinds of trouble together. Mark still has a love for trouble, but mostly the kind that involves smoking weed and drinking too much beer."

I laughed and leaned closer so he could hear me. "You're good at finding the perfect places and people. Thanks, this is exactly what I needed."

We hung out and listened to The Smoky Rags for several hours, catching a beer between their songs and getting to know the band. Turned out The Rags were a few college-age kids playing gigs all around the western part of the state and Mark had agreed to help them with their first CD.

I asked to be their first customer. The band was actually really good, and I thought their music would be great for banging down the road when you needed a heavy beat and some loud music to drive your troubles away.

We left in good spirits, me tipsy and Joseph, the very responsible driver who managed to nurse his Bud for the entire afternoon, sober and clearly pleased that I'd enjoyed the ambiance and music.

"You still up for a little more fun?" he asked.

"Get me some Ibuprofen, and I'll be good to go for the rest of the night," I said.

"I can do that. Want to come see my place? It's a drive, but if you're up for it, I'd love to have you stay with me tonight."

A thrill passed through me that left me speechless for a moment. I swallowed hard. "Do you mind stopping at Beth's first so I can grab some clean clothes and a toothbrush?"

"Sure. It's on the way," he said cheerfully.

So, what if I sucked at keeping things simple. If the man wanted me to spend my first night out of a cast snuggled up in his arms, doing things he'd promised to do a few nights ago, who was I to stop him? Shit, I'd been able to think of nothing else but his promise... or more accurately, the threat he'd made that night. No fucking way was I going to pass that opportunity up.

"Just so you know," Joseph added, "I have no intention of this being *the night*, but I'd really like you to see my place, and I can do a lot with you that doesn't involve us going all the way."

"I'm not opposed to all the way," I whispered.

He laughed out loud. "No, but I'm not done romancing you. You asked me to make sure our friendship was solid before we went on to sex, and I agreed. I'm an honest man, and my integrity means a lot to me, so I will keep my promise. That doesn't mean I won't take things right up to that line. Besides, what kind of friend would I be if I didn't make you beg a little?"

"No kind of friend I've ever had before, that's for damned sure," I said, and he laughed.

Joseph's place was small but full of character. The original one-room cabin had been added onto several times, giving it a rambling effect. The thing that gave this cabin its true glory was the proximity to the water. It sat upon a small peninsula that jutted out several hundred feet from the main shoreline. It was clear why the original settlers picked the spot because the higher side of the peninsula faced the Salish Sea and protected the lower cove. There was a small drop to the sea on that side, but a ramp had been built down to the beach and where it stopped was a sweet little dock.

Joseph told me the water here was deep and that Peter could moor his sailboat right next to the dock without fear of running aground. Navigating out into the sea was a bit trickier, as the entire inlet was littered with undersea boulders that would happily rip the bottom out of a boat. The only reason Peter risked it was because he had sonar that guided him through the area.

Joseph talked about the local history, including a legend that the area was once used by the natives.

"The property has passed through several hands, but the last owner donated it to the Tribe. I'm allowed to live here because the previous occupant knew me and put me in his will. It's sort of like a life estate."

The cabin rambled. There was an old kitchen that was clearly remodeled in the nineteen fifties or sixties, equipped with an old wood-burning stove. The furniture wasn't much newer, and the entire place felt as though it had been thrust back in time. Despite the lack of modern amenities, the property was charming and had a feeling of magic about it. Joseph saw me looking his kitchen over and laughed.

"You can guess I don't do much cooking in here," he said.

I asked if he would be allowed to remodel, and he said that his agreement with the Tribe had no end date allotted, so as long as he kept the property up, he guessed he'd be allowed to do what he wanted.

"I think in your situation, I'd do that remodel sooner than later, but honestly, Joseph, your place looks like something out of a fairy tale. Thank you for bringing me out to see it."

I sat down on the well-worn, but incredibly comfortable sofa and Joseph brought over a beer for each of us.

"Sorry, I don't have a TV here, just some old records from the previous occupant." He shrugged.

"No worries," I said. "I'm just enjoying your company and seeing where you live. This place really does represent you well."

"Oh," he laughed. "Is that so? What does it show you?"

I smiled and hesitated. I didn't want to offend him, but I made a stab at it anyway.

"Since I met you, it's clear you're a man that appreciates his privacy. I also sense that you prefer to be as close to nature as you can get. This place allows you to be as close as possible without living in a tent. It also just feels like you—" I paused, wanting to say more.

"You have more insight?" Joseph asked.

"Maybe more than I should share at this point. I'm not ready to scare you off quite yet."

"I'm doubting you can, but why don't you try," Joseph chuckled.

Throwing caution to the wind, I confessed my thoughts, "since I was a little boy, I've had what Southern people call 'the sight.' I don't really 'see things,' so to speak, but I can sense them. This place feels like you, and it feels like someone else too. In fact, when I really pay attention, I can feel several people all at once. This is a very happy place, one that screams solitude but also sings peace and tranquility." I was embarrassed that I'd disclosed so much of myself. "I don't tell people that, Joseph, I got a little carried away."

Joseph leaned over and kissed me. "Don't apologize. I'm glad you shared it with me. Since I'm descended from the natives of this area, I am not afraid of things not proven by science. Who knows, I might have a few secrets myself."

"Oh," I responded, intrigued, "what might those be?"

Joseph chuckled again. "I prefer to let secrets express themselves when the time is right. For now, know that sharing your gifts with me just makes me want to know you better."

Joseph had clearly thought ahead, and there was cold fried chicken, potato salad and some vegetable medley for dinner. After that, he grabbed a couple towels, and we hiked through the woods to a small hot spring-fed pool.

"You are full of surprises!" I exclaimed at the sight of the pool.

"It came with the property," he said.

"Only one problem," I added, "I didn't bring a suit."

"That won't be a problem here," he said, cocking a naughty eyebrow toward me. "You're safe. The only people I ever see up here are the occasional ranger, and they only come to visit me. There isn't anyone planning to visit tonight."

"So, this is your way to get me naked?"

"You got me," he laughed.

We stripped and climbed gingerly into the hot pool. Once we'd got used to the heat, Joseph waded over and kissed me.

"This pool is thought to have healing qualities. My ancestors used this as a place of medicine long before Europeans arrived. I thought it would be a good place for you to soak that newly freed arm of yours."

I was taken aback by Joseph's thoughtful gesture. He'd really thought of everything. I had thought he'd pulled me out to this incredibly romantic spot to loosen me up for sex, which, as far as I was concerned, still wasn't out of the question. But he was also thinking about me... *still* thinking about me.

That made me feel vulnerable and just a bit emotional. I ducked under the water to avoid him seeing the tears that were burning the backs of my eyes, but when I came back up, Joseph was still there looking at me. I reached for him, pulling him to me and kissed him hard.

"You make me feel things, Joseph. That scares me and thrills me all at the same time. I've... I've never met anyone like you."

Joseph didn't respond but rather pulled me closer and kissed me back. Surprising me, he took my arm and began massaging it, then doing what appeared to be physical therapy. I asked him where he'd learned to do that, and he laughed.

"We all know how to search the internet. I also asked a physical therapist friend of mine what should and shouldn't be done with your arm at this point. She also approved of the hot water treatment."

I guess the thing that surprised me the most about our time in the pool was that I was able to resist jumping him. The only thing that saved me was that Joseph was intent on helping me recover. Had he shown even a glimmer of interest in sex, I'd have been all over him. I was beginning to regret asking him to be a friend before we had sex.

I wanted nothing more than to worship Joseph's body with my tongue. I could only imagine the taste of him as he glistened in the heat of the pool, with the smell of the forest on his skin. It didn't pay to ponder such things. The water was cloudy, but my interest in Joseph couldn't be hidden completely.

By the time we got back to the cabin, I was unfortunately done in. I'd expected all the work Joseph did on my arm to leave me hurting, but in fact, I had no pain in my arm at all.

"I don't know what your plans for the night were, but between the beers, the hot tub, and the stuff around my arm, I'm tuckered out," I said and smiled at him.

Joseph put his arm around me and kissed me again.

"I had plans to make you feel special and cared about. I expected you'd be tired, and I already told you, I didn't expect tonight to be *the night*."

We went into his bedroom, and I was asleep about as fast as I laid down. I knew Joseph had laid down next to me, but only in that glimmer of knowledge that occurs just before you fall asleep. I guess I must have slept pretty hard because I woke up the next morning not knowing where I was. When I remembered I was at Joseph's, I realized his arms were wrapped around me, and he was breathing softly into my neck. I stirred, trying not to wake him, but having to pee bad enough that staying in bed was no longer an option.

I managed to slip out of his arms, but my movement must have woken him, and he was feeling around for me, groaning slightly at having lost the heat of my body next to his.

I did my business and returned to a semi-conscious Joseph, who smiled at my arrival.

"Did you sleep well?" he asked.

"I slept as hard as something between a rock and a mountain. Did you drug me or something?"

He laughed. "The water in the pool sometimes has that effect on people. How does your arm feel?"

"It feels fine, but I really need to get it back in its sling before I end up doing too much."

Joseph agreed, and after we'd showered, I secured the soft cast, and we headed back into town for breakfast. Joseph had to help his dad that morning, so we were both expected at the workshop.

We arrived at Kaden's around eleven, just in time to see Sam Jeffs step out of the house.

I looked over at Joseph, not knowing what his reaction would be, but I could see from his face that it wasn't a negative one. Sam waved at us as she started her car and pulled out of the driveway.

"Is this the first time you've seen your dad date someone?" I asked.

"Well, yes and no. I've met a couple of women Dad took out, but to the best of my knowledge, this is the first time he's gotten serious enough with one to have her stay over at his place. I'd be lying if I said I'm not a little overwhelmed by it all, but at the same time, I know my mom wouldn't want him to live the rest of his life alone."

He stared out the window for a moment before saying, "Besides, I like Sam."

"Well," I added, "one thing is for sure, she really seems to like him. I think if it were dark, that woman would be glowing."

Joseph smiled. "Yep, we McCoys do know how to satisfy our lovers."

I cringed. "As much as I hope that's true on your part, I would rather not think that thought about your dad."

Joseph thought my discomfort was hilarious. "What, you don't want me to be a great lover?" Having had enough of the conversation, I jumped out of the car and headed to the door.

"As for how good a lover you are, I'll be the judge of that when the time comes." I said as he came up behind me.

I pushed my way through the door and saw Kaden coming down the stairs, clearly in a good mood.

Joseph began teasing his dad. "Was that Sam Jeffs coming out of the house when we pulled up?"

"You know damned well it was. Now tend to your own business."

"Seems like if you're going to turn that woman into my step-mom, it might be my business."

"I haven't said anything about turning anyone into anything. If I decide to marry the woman, then you can get your nose all out of joint, till then mind your own."

Clearly, Kaden was in no mood to discuss his love life with us. Knowing he'd taken the joke as far as he could without repercussions, Joseph backed off, and we all started planning how best to get the first project done for the Seattle mansion.

The day's project was a modern style buffet with a mix of maple, steel, and glass. From Kaden's drawing, it was going to be something beautiful. I had no idea where they would even start, so I went back to answering the phones and sweeping up sawdust. I paid close attention to how they used the tools in the workshop and thought, with time, I could probably learn to use them as well. Of course, it wouldn't hurt to have both hands back in working order.

The week passed too quickly, and before I knew it, I was headed back to Seattle and away from the only place I'd been happy since leaving my family in Tennessee.

Paul and Jeff met me at the door when I pulled into the driveway, and grabbed me into a hug. It was both nice and strange. We were not a hugging kind of family. Jeff had cooked up a huge welcome home meal. Unfortunately, my appetite was all but gone. The thought of going into court and having to come face to face with that jackass Nathan was all I could stomach. The boys could see I was pretty much done for, and after dinner, they helped carry my things up to my room.

Court was everything I knew it would be and dreaded.

Mr. McAllister and Nathan sat together on the other side of the room from me. The case was called. Nathan went on the stand and made up a whole bunch of nonsense about how I'd been harassing him since I'd hit him in the nose. I looked over at my former boss to see if he was gonna contradict the fabricated tale Nathan was spinning, but he didn't, and he never took his eyes off Nathan. Lies or truth wouldn't matter there. Mr. McAllister was in Nathan's court and would only support him.

Nathan was asking the court for a restraining order and that I also be held in jail until his safety could be ensured. As he continued making up all kinds of stories, there was nothing I could do but watch. I shook my head and blushed both out of humiliation and absolute anger.

What happened next shook me and restored my faith in humanity.

I heard a voice coming from the back of the courtroom. "I'm sorry I'm late, Your Honor. I was held up with the Owens case."

"Mr. Riley, who are you here to represent?"

Todd looked at me and smiled. "One moment, Your Honor. I need to do a little housekeeping, then I'll answer that question."

I smiled. "Todd, what are you doing here?"

Todd whispered back, "If you sign this paper, I'm thinking I might save your ass."

"Todd, I appreciate it, but I don't have any money to pay you."

"Do you have a dollar on you?" Todd asked

"No, but I have a five," I replied, confused.

"Hand me the five and sign this document." Confused, I did as he instructed.

Todd turned to the judge and said, "Your Honor, I'm here to represent Daniel Porter.

The judge looked at me, then at Todd, and finally over to Nathan.

"Mr. Hastings, do you have an objection to counsel?" Nathan looked confused and angry but shook his head.

"I don't think so, but if he is going to have an attorney, I need one too."

"That's a great idea, young man. So, unless there is an objection, I'm going to continue this case and set the next date for three weeks. Young man, you need to bring your attorney with you the next time we have court." The bailiff worked with Todd and Nathan to set up a time for the next hearing, and we were dismissed.

As we walked out of the courtroom, Nathan confronted me and demanded to know why I'd hired an attorney.

Todd stepped in between Nathan and me. "Simply because he has the right to one. If you don't mind, I would ask that you do not make contact with my client again until after the trial. If you have any questions or when you get your own attorney, they may contact me at this number."

Todd handed his card to Nathan, put his hand on my shoulder and led me out of the courtroom.

"Under no circumstances are you to talk to him. Do you understand me, Daniel?" Todd said in a firm voice.

"No worries there," I said. "I'd be happy if I never have to set eyes on that man again."

"Well, unfortunately," Todd said, "that isn't going to be the case. You will see him again in three weeks. Until then, I need you to stay clear. Do you know of any place you could go that would allow you to get away? Somewhere this guy can't find you?" Todd gave me a knowing look.

"I may have a place I could go," I said and smiled. "I'm glad you rescued me. Nathan was making shit up left and right in there. I had no idea how I was going to defend myself against any of that. I'm only happy you distracted him long enough that he couldn't get the restraining order put on my record."

"That was actually when I decided to intervene," Todd admitted. "I'd slipped into the courtroom to see how you were progressing, and the more that jackass talked, the more I realized he was hell-bent on putting you away."

I sighed as the reality of the situation set in.

"I appreciate this, Todd, but I really can't afford you. Seriously, I lost my job as a result of all this crap, and I'd rather go to jail than ask my brother for money."

Todd winked at me and said, "Well, luckily for you, my husband and I are looking for a fly fish caddie."

I turned to Todd and laughed. "A what?"

"A fly fish caddie. Like a golf caddie but for fly fishing."

"Todd," I laughed. "That isn't a thing."

Todd reached inside his briefcase, pulled out the contract I'd just signed and asked, "Did you read this?"

I shrugged. "I didn't really have much time for that."

"Well, you better read it now. Apparently, there *is* such a thing, and you just agreed to be Mac's and my caddie for a total of twenty hours. That would be about two full weekends."

I couldn't do anything but laugh. "Does Mac know you contracted a nincompoop to be your flyfishing caddie?"

"Who do you think came up with the idea?" Todd asked.

"You're both nuts," I replied. "But I am sure glad you are. Todd, I can't thank you enough for this."

Todd turned a sly smile on me. "Don't thank me, we intend to drag your butt all through the Olympic Mountains. By the time we're done, you're going to be a fly fisherman, and once you get the addiction, we'll have at least one gay friend to go with us on these excursions."

"So," I replied, "this is a conspiracy to convert me into an outdoorsy queen."

Todd touched his nose and grinned. "You catch on fast."

He told me he had another couple of cases before lunch and to meet him at his office in an hour to go over the case.

"I want to know what we are up against. I have part of the story from you, and Joseph filled me in on parts of it, but I need to know from you what actually happened."

I stopped by a coffee shop on the way and grabbed two lattes, remembering that Todd had brought a thermos of latte with him when they went fishing. When I arrived at Todd's office, I was impressed by the layout, it was modern but small. Todd was obviously in private practice, which was probably why he could be so generous with me.

He invited me into his office, and I sat across from him. He wanted all the details from the night of the incident, so I told him everything that happened from start to finish.

When I was done rehashing the story, Todd whistled.

"It seems your friend is blowing this way out of proportion. Do you think he'll be able to get witnesses like your ex and your former boss?"

I shrugged. "It's possible. I think Mr. McAllister has a crush on Nathan. He was in court with him today. My ex, Tony, is a block of meat. I can't predict what he'll say or do."

"So, we will have to use his lies against him then. He is already on record saying that you have harassed him since you had the incident. Have you had any contact with him through Facebook, text, anything?"

"No, I blocked him on my phone and all my social media. I also unfriended everyone who was friends with both of us, not that I've been on Facebook that often since the event. You can go through all my social media and see I haven't posted or even messaged anyone since I fell off the mountain. Besides, Nathan hasn't tried to text or call me either, so there's been no contact," I said.

"That's good," Todd smiled. "We can use that to impeach him. Meanwhile, I want you back in Port Angeles. I've already called Joseph, and he said Beth was willing to put you back up."

I moaned. "I'm not willing to take advantage of poor Beth any longer," I said. "I'm going to try to get a cheap hotel room or something while I'm there."

"I'll let you work all that out," Todd said. "But if I'm right, and I usually am, that man is going to make a move to get you into deep trouble. I've been around the block a few times, and you have a real enemy there, Daniel. You need to watch your back. I know I'd feel a lot better if you were nowhere near him."

"I'll work it out," I assured him. "Besides, I think Kaden needs an assistant. If I can convince him of that, I think I'll have work. Even at minimum wage, that should cover a nice enough hotel room at least until I'm done with this whole court thing."

Todd and I shook hands, and I left, agreeing to let him know when I returned to the Peninsula.

Both Paul and Jeff were home when I got back from court. I cocked an eyebrow at them. "So, neither of you had work today?"

They both shrugged, then Jeff walked out of the room when Paul began attacking me for information. "You should have just come with me if you were going to be like this about it," I said.

"You didn't invite me, or I would have," Paul said, his own Southern accent slipping out, which only tended to show itself when he was upset, angry or tired.

"Next time, I promise to invite you," I said, and Paul cringed.

"So, there is a next time?" he asked.

"Yeah, but Joseph's friend rescued me from what would've been a disaster. Once again, Joseph saved my ass."

I shook my head, then remembered I hadn't told my brother about Joseph. When I looked over at him, I could tell he was about to burst from not asking me questions.

"Go ahead," I said. "You're going to have a stroke if you don't ask." I could hear Jeff laughing from the other room.

"Okay, so who is Joseph?" Paul asked, trying to be nonchalant.

I sighed and sat down, encouraging Paul to sit as well. "Joseph is probably the prettiest man who ever walked the Pacific Northwest, and he thinks I'm cute." Then I embarrassed myself by giggling like a little girl.

Jeff walked back into the living room to join Paul and me. I'm guessing the discussion of pretty Joseph was what it took to get him to discard his veiled attempt to give us space. It was just as well. Paul and Jeff were a unit, I don't even know why they pretended to be otherwise. Everyone in our family saw them that way now. One didn't exist outside the other.

Both Jeff and Paul, who were now sitting side by side on the sofa across from me, stared like little children waiting for a parent to return to telling them a bedtime story.

I knew there was nothing to do but spit out everything that had happened since I'd left a month earlier.

"Joseph was on the team of rescuers who brought my broken ass off the mountain. Then, although I thought it'd been the nurse from the hospital, it was him who set it up for me to be taken to Beth's place. She is his aunt."

"Oh," Paul said, "that makes a lot more sense."

"Yeah," I continued. "My knight in shining armor rescued me both times. While I was there, Joseph and I became close. Very close," I added for effect, "but before you get that worried look on your face, we haven't done anything other than kiss. Well, I guess we did technically sleep together, but that is all we did. Not that I didn't want to do more." Realizing who I was talking to, my face blushed.

"Forget that last part, I digress. Anyway, in court today, Nathan was up first. He was making up shit left and right about how I was harassing him since the incident and that he needed court protection from me. Then Joseph's attorney friend, Todd, who I met while up there, showed up out of the blue and announced he was taking my case. Which is a good thing because if it had progressed as it was going, I'd probably be serving a twenty-year sentence or something."

"Dang," my brother-in-law said. "I knew he was a weasel, but I had no idea he was that evil. I still don't understand why he wants to take you down so bad."

"That makes two of us," I agreed. "I know I embarrassed him when I punched him in the face but seriously, he did have it coming. Who sticks their tongue down their so-called friend's boyfriend's throat?"

"Especially when they know you're coming into work," Paul said quietly.

I hadn't considered that part. I looked over at Paul. "You think this was on purpose?" I asked.

"Could be," Paul said. "I, like Jeff, knew something wasn't quite right about the guy. He seemed more interested in upping you than being a friend, but you were happy hanging out with him." Paul looked at his husband and shrugged. "We both knew you were struggling with friendships, so we looked the other way instead of saying something. I'm sorry, Daniel. We shouldn't have looked the other way."

I could see that Paul was upset and feeling guilty.

"Paul, you have no reason to feel guilty. I'm the one who's a bad judge of character. Besides, I have you two, and that's more than most people have." Then I sighed and put my good hand up in the air. "Okay, that got sappy. Too much for my Southern sensibilities to handle." As I walked out of the room, both Paul and Jeff were chuckling.

Jeff yelled out, "It's about time you two let a little Yankee percolate into those emotionally-deprived blocks you carry around."

"Whatever," both Paul and I said in unison.

Before I was out of the room, I turned back around. "My new attorney said I need to make myself scarce until the trial. I'm going to go back up to Port Angeles, I think." My brother frowned but nodded.

"I think he's probably right. If Nathan is out to get you, he is more likely than not going to try to set you up. I don't like that you're having to leave your home, but you seemed happy there anyway. I think it's best if you just extend your vacation a little longer."

When I got to my room, I called Joseph and asked him if he could help me find a cheap hotel or even an apartment to rent for the next few weeks. Before he asked, I told him I didn't want to take advantage of him or his family, so it needed to be a place I could pay for out of my meager savings. He agreed to help me look.

"I have another question," I told him before hanging up. "Do you think your dad would be willing to hire me part-time to help him get the office put back in order while I'm there? I need a job, and he seems to need the help."

Joseph laughed and said he would almost be willing to hire me to do the job so his dad would leave him alone, but he promised to ask. We talked a bit more and confirmed we were happy to have more time together. I didn't want to get mushy, though, so I jumped off the call before it went into the *I miss you* stuff.

Within an hour, I'd got a call from Kaden. When I answered, he simply said, "Yes. When will you be back?"

I laughed in spite of myself. "I'm going to stay the weekend at my brother's, but I can drive up Sunday night and stay in a hotel until I find an apartment."

"No," he said firmly. "I'm afraid that last part isn't going to work. Beth is about to blow a gasket. When Joseph told her you were coming up, she demanded you stay there. Son, I'm afraid you aren't going to get out of this one, and none of us are brave enough to challenge her. She can be a demon when she puts her mind to something."

"Mr. McCoy, sir," I said. "That is me taking advantage of her, and I can't do that."

"Young man, you don't have a choice, seriously." He laughed and hung up the phone after confirming he'd see me on Monday morning.

I dialed Beth's number next. I was ready to win this battle, knowing Beth was doing this to make me feel better, but she answered much like Kaden did with no introduction. "Can you afford five-hundred dollars?"

"Huh?" I asked, completely taken off guard.

"Can you afford five-hundred dollars for the month?" she asked again.

"I think so," I stammered, then tried to argue. "But Mrs. Beth, that isn't enough, and you have guests."

"That is enough because that is what I asked for. I don't want other guests, I want you. Hell, I just about brought you back from the dead myself. At least this way, I can see your healing all the way through to the end. Besides, I miss you and enjoy watching how you make Joseph all goofy when he's around. I'm thinking about turning your story into a straight romance novel."

I couldn't help but laugh at that. "Okay, I can agree to that, but I get to be the guy and I want to be all butch and handsome." I could hear Beth laughing out loud as she put her hand over the mouthpiece of her phone.

When she came back, she said matter of factly, "As if you were the guy in this story."

Before I could stop myself, I blurted out, "Bitch." Before I could apologize, she just chuckled and said, "Oh, honey, you have no idea."

"God help me," I responded. "You're going to turn me into some trollop, aren't you?"

"You call me a bitch again, and you'll see what I turn you into." Then she laughed for a long time before she asked, "When will you be back up?"

"I told Kaden I'd be at work on Monday. Is Sunday night okay?" I asked.

"That will be perfect," she said and disconnected as quickly as she'd answered. I would never get used to the way people up here got on and off phone conversations so quickly. When I called my family, there was at least fifteen minutes on either side of the real conversation for civil bullshit. I never planned a phone call with any of them for less than an hour.

Paul and Jeff took me with them to a gallery opening a friend of theirs was having on Saturday. They didn't really take no for an answer. I assumed they wanted to keep an eye on me just to make sure the idiot Nathan never had access. Halfway through the evening, Jeff's phone went off, indicating that someone had tried to break into the house. The alarm company called and said the police were on their way.

When we arrived home, the police were still there. The door was standing ajar, and the police were dusting for fingerprints. So far, they had lifted a few prints, and we were told we needed to go down to the station so they could compare our prints to the ones found. Then they allowed us to go inside and check if anything was missing. We wandered around the first level, and nothing seemed to be out of place. Paul and Jeff went up to their room, and I followed behind. When I walked into my room, everything had been tossed. Worse yet, it looked like the perp had taken a knife to my clothing. Several pairs of my underwear had the crotch cut out of them.

"Guys," I hollered across the hall. "I think I have a clue who did this."

When they came into my room, Paul drew in a breath. He walked back out into the hall and called for the officers to come upstairs and showed them the mess. Paul and Jeff's friend, Cliff Sparks, the officer who'd arrested me for the incident that happened in Seattle, beat the Edmonds Police up the stairs.

Jeff must have called him after receiving the alarm company's notification about the break-in.

He looked at my room, at Jeff, and then at me. "I'm assuming this is your room," he said to me.

I nodded, not trusting that I had a voice.

"Who do you think would do this?" he asked.

Paul chimed in then. "We know who did this. It was that sorry, no good, piece of"

Jeff interrupted Paul before he got wound up. "It was probably Nathan. The man Daniel allegedly hit." Then Jeff looked at me and elaborated. "They had court yesterday, and Daniel showed up with an attorney. Apparently, that really pissed him off."

"Apparently," one of the other policemen who'd followed Officer Cliff up from below agreed. "Have you seen this guy since court?"

"No," I managed to say. "I've been with my attorney or with my brother and Jeff the entire time. They can vouch for my whereabouts."

"Okay," the officer said. "You three need to come down and have your prints taken. I doubt we'll find any others, but if we do, we'll at least have a lead."

"Will you question Nathan?" Jeff asked the officer.

"I'm sorry, sir, I can't comment on investigation specifics, but I can promise we won't leave any rock unturned. This is especially concerning. People don't usually attack personal items like this unless they mean to scare someone, or worse."

The officer looked at me meaningfully. "You need to watch your back," he said.

"Want me to call our cousins?" Paul asked, clearly getting angrier by the minute. "No doubt they could take care of this."

I glanced at Paul, startled that he'd even ask such a question. That side of the family was... intense. My grandfather's brothers and their kids were in and out of prison for any number of things. They weren't afraid of anything or anyone and that included the law.

More than a few bad apples had disappeared from our county after having harassed or hurt someone in our family and even though they were never charged, it was common knowledge our cousins were behind it.

Jeff looked at Paul, his eyes wide, and then at his police friend. "No, we won't be calling your cousins. Cliff will fix this the legal way," he concluded. Cliff was smiling when he left. He knew Paul, but he obviously didn't know our cousins. That was probably for the best. If he knew what we knew, he'd probably have arrested both of us just for being related to them.

Paul stomped over to his bedroom, with Jeff close behind. The cops took pictures of my room. I couldn't handle them snapping photos of my ripped, crotchless underwear, so I wandered over to Paul and Jeff's room and leaned on the doorframe. Jeff was consoling Paul, who was clearly ready to kill someone. I hadn't seen my brother this way, at least not in a long time. He was always so well put together, but I guess you can take the man out of the South, but the Southern protective spirit that dwells in our souls can never be taken out of us, at least not completely.

"I'm okay, Paul," I said and got a look that usually only came from our mother. I shrunk under the look just as Paul shook it off.

"You are going to get out of town, that's for damned sure. We are going to have the Edmonds Police let the Sheriff's Office in Port Angeles know to keep an eye out for that maniac." Then Paul looked at Jeff and said, "This is why we don't have guns. I think I could kill that motherfucker myself."

Both Jeff and I looked at my brother in shock. Who was this guy?

Jeff took my brother's hand. "Daniel will be just fine. This was a prank, the idiot wanted to get him in court, and when he lost his opportunity, he decided to act like a terrorist. There is no need to give him the satisfaction of winning. If he comes back, you can knock him in the head with your frying pan or rolling pin or whatever other Southern thing you guys hit each other with when you're ready to kill each other."

Paul smiled, which was obviously what Jeff was working toward. Once again, I was struck by how perfect the two of them were for each other. Their love seemed to be exactly what the other needed. Paul reached over and kissed Jeff, then turned to me.

"I love you, Daniel, but I'll feel safer when you're out of the city. I think Jeff is right that Nathan just wants to scare you, but if he is dangerous, I'd prefer you to be safe."

"I'm going tomorrow. I'd like to see that idiot take on Mrs. Beth. She'd rip him limb to limb."

Paul smiled, remembering her. "I'm sure she could, but you make sure she knows about all this too, just in case. I don't want her getting any nasty surprises."

"I will," I promised.

"Now, let's go down to the station and get this fingerprinting crap done and over with."

As the officer had predicted, the prints only matched ours. Nathan must've worn gloves.

I didn't get much sleep that night. I stayed up and salvaged what clothing hadn't been ripped up or taken for evidence by the police department. The rest, I threw in a trash bag and took out to the curb where I noticed a car parked down the block, engine running, but the lights were off. *You are becoming paranoid.* Though, I quickly returned to the house, just in case. I managed to get a few hours' sleep with the help of one of my remaining prescribed painkillers, but I got up early and met my brother and Jeff for breakfast and a cup of coffee. I told them my plans for the drive up and that I'd call them when I got to Beth's house.

When I pulled out of the driveway, I noticed the same car from the night before. This time, it pulled into traffic just as I put the car in drive and moved forward. I decided to be safer than sorry and called the police. I told them I thought the person who broke into my home last night may be following me, then took a few sideroads until they showed up. When they did, they pulled the car over and I pulled forward and waited for them to come talk to me.

An officer finally came up to my side of the car and when I rolled the window down, he confirmed that the guy was following me. "He claims he's a private investigator who was hired by your friend to follow you and figure out what you were up to. Those were his words, not mine."

"Damn," I said. "Is there any way I can get out of here before that jackass follows me to where I'm going? My attorney wants me away from anyone until after we have court."

"No problem, we're taking the guy in for questioning since he was following you the day after someone broke into your home and knifed your clothing. That is something we don't let slide without getting a lot of questions answered."

"Thank you, officer," I said. "By the way, did anyone find out where my so-called friend was last night?"

"I'm not sure," the officer said. "I don't have all the information on your case, but you can call the station, and someone should be able to fill you in on what, if anything, was found."

I thanked the officer again and slipped into traffic, making sure no one followed me this time.

When I arrived at Beth's, the entire gang was there waiting for me. Strangely, it was more like coming home than when I'd gone home to Paul and Jeff's. It made me wonder what it was about the place that made it feel so right. Tennessee was nothing like this area. Sure, it was a small town like the one I'd grown up in, but the people were progressive and much more forward-thinking. No one seemed to care if you liked men or women. It was more of a small town with a big city point of view.

Also, there was something about the area, about the family, that was different, and I couldn't quite put my finger on it.

On my way back, I'd stopped at a Fred Meyer department store and bought a couple new packs of underwear and a couple new shirts as well as a few pairs of jeans. That should do me well working on a construction site, I thought.

When I walked into the house, I was first met by Joseph, who grabbed me into a big hug then kissed me square on the lips.

"Oh, that was quite a wonderful way to be greeted," I said to him. Then I kissed him back but with more relish.

Kaden cleared his throat, and I looked up to see him and Beth both looking at us with the kind of look a parent gives a child when they've snuck a cookie out of the cookie jar.

"Well, at least you know Joseph is happy to see you," Beth retorted and giggled as she headed toward the kitchen.

Kaden didn't move away. Instead, he asked, "Young man, what are your intentions with my son?"

I didn't know what the hell to say to that, so I shrugged and answered honestly. "To kiss him a lot more?"

Both Kaden and Joseph laughed at my answer.

"Good answer," Kaden said and went back into the living room with the rest of their family.

I walked into the kitchen where Beth was and hugged her. "I hope this isn't an inconvenience. I didn't want to take advantage of you, Mrs. Beth," I said.

"Nonsense, I want you here, and it feels great to have you back home," she replied.

"Thank you. It means a lot to me to be here. It *felt* like I was coming home."

Beth beamed at me. "As it should, Daniel, as it should. Now, come on into the living room. Everyone from the family is here, including Joseph's Uncle Evan. He's keen to meet you since you're dating his favorite nephew."

"Wait, are there any other nephews?" I asked.

"Nope," she replied. "He's the only one."

"I see, thus, the favorite," I chuckled.

"You are a quick one," she said, and pulled me into the living room with her.

When I walked in, I was astonished. Evan was indeed a beautiful man. When Beth had used that word to describe her late husband, Evan's twin William, I wasn't thinking she literally meant he could be a model in any magazine of his choosing. As was the custom with his family, Evan had a hundred questions, ranging from my childhood to my career choices. I'd gone through similar questioning with Martha and Kaden when I met them, so I wasn't surprised.

Evan talked a little about his clinic in Oregon and about how he was considering the big retirement. His husband was several years older than him, and they were both hungry to do more traveling before they got too old to enjoy it.

So far, I'd met and liked everyone in Joseph's family, so that was good, I thought. Although, I wasn't sure how much you were supposed to get attached to someone's family when you were just beginning to date them.

Date? Were we even considering that? Maybe I needed to check myself before I jumped the gun. See, this was why you didn't meet the family until after you'd decided you were in a relationship with someone. As it was, I felt like I was already in a relationship with the family, and I hadn't even slept with Joseph yet. Okay, I know, yes, I had slept with him but not *slept* with him.

Joseph must have noticed I was in my head because he drew the attention back to me. "So how long do you plan to stay, Daniel?" he asked.

"I'm here for at least three weeks," I responded. "Then I'm not sure. A lot of that might depend on whether my new employer decides to fire me or not."

Kaden winked at me. "If you can keep all those pesky phone calls away from me, we should be golden forever."

I laughed and fully understood what he meant. The phone at Kaden's office literally rang constantly.

"How's your arm been feeling now that your cast is off?" Beth asked.

"I still have issues, and the doc said I couldn't really use it much for another few weeks. At least I don't have that horrible cast on any longer, and the pain is manageable. I should be getting more movement and use out of it as the weeks pass."

Beth had ordered dinner from the local supermarket again, and after we'd eaten, I excused myself and headed up to my room. Joseph came with me and helped carry my luggage. After placing the cases on the bed, he turned toward me and melted every bone in my body when his lips met mine.

"I want to do that all the time," he said. "I was totally jealous of my family down there. I kept thinking, when can I get you alone so I could kiss you again."

I laughed at him and put my hand on his chest. "I have thought of little else since I last saw you. I keep forcing myself to behave so I don't scare you off. I could become a totally obsessed Joseph fan if I don't work hard to avoid it."

"Mmm," Joseph moaned. "I want you to be the number one Joseph fan. When do we get to have groupie sex?"

Dear God, I was hard as a rock, and the man had barely touched me. "I'd say right now, except I think your entire family is sitting downstairs, and that feels too weird."

"I could go ask them all to leave," Joseph said.

"Yeah, and that wouldn't lead to future issues at all, would it?" I asked, laughing. Joseph laughed too.

"Okay, you have a point. Why don't we go to my place tomorrow night? I think you need more hot springs, and I need more you time," he said as he snuggled me into his arms.

"You don't have to ask me twice," I moaned. "Now, go before I jump you right here and now and end up embarrassing us both."

Joseph smiled at me and walked toward the door. "Think about this while I'm gone. You know the promise I made you last time we talked?" I nodded, a lump collecting in my throat. "Tomorrow night, I make good on that promise."

I gulped and swallowed hard and I just about managed to squeak, "Okay…"

Joseph's smile turned more sly, and he winked at me before he left my room. As he walked out, he said, "I'll pick you up after you're done working with Dad."

Dear God, I thought my heart would explode out of my chest, and if I didn't have on baggy sweat pants, I'm sure something more embarrassing would've burst out of them. I truly wanted to get Joseph naked, and to be honest, was more than a little surprised we hadn't had sex already, but I had to admit the playful anticipation was making it that much more appealing. I was going to enjoy touching and licking Joseph McCoy's body from top to bottom.

I fell asleep thinking about Joseph's promise… or threat. Either way, I couldn't wait until tomorrow night.

There was definitely something about this place because I usually never remembered my dreams. But when I was here, it's like they were real and not dreams at all.

I was standing not far from the hot springs next to Joseph's place. There was a mist covering the ground, except for the pool.

I could feel myself being pulled toward the them, I took off and found myself flying instead of walking.

I knew, more than saw, that I was the owl this time. As I neared the springs, I spotted Joseph floating face up in the water. When he saw me, he smiled and stood up, welcoming me to him.

All around us the mists chanted in indistinguishable languages and when I landed, I was no longer the owl, but rather myself again. I walked into the water and into my lover's arms, knowing something important had happened just then. Somehow our souls had called out to each other and now as we embraced, we were becoming one.

I woke up early and met Kaden just as he was pulling up to Beth's home. "Good morning," I said, jumping into his truck.

"Why are you so chipper?" Kaden asked.

"Well, if you must know, I have two reasons. One, I'm looking forward to learning more about your business, and two, I have a date with your son tonight."

Kaden looked over at me with a cocked eyebrow. "You two are getting serious, then?"

"Hell no," I said. "This is really only like our third date. There are laws about getting serious until like the fifth or sixth date."

Kaden laughed. "You know my son doesn't play by those rules, right?"

"What do you mean?" I asked.

Kaden thought for a moment. "I'm just going to say that Joseph isn't one to play games. If he likes you, he likes you, and he wouldn't be going out with you unless that was the case. I know I may be playing my dad card a little early. Just promise me this, if you decide you don't want this to go any further than dating, you'll break it off with him sooner than later. He has the kind of heart that could easily be broken."

My first reaction was a bit of a freak out, but fuck... this was his freaking dad. Of course, he's making more of this than I was ready to. I shook off the discomfort and reached over, put my hand on Kaden's shoulder and squeezed.

"I know he's special, and I know he isn't a player or at least I know that now. I can't promise I'm going to be his husband or anything, but I can say this, I won't ever hurt him intentionally."

"Then," Kaden said, "that is all a dad can ask for." He hesitated a moment and then added, "Just keep in mind that he'll need his space, okay? I think that might be the hardest part of dating someone like Joseph."

With that, we pulled out of Beth's driveway. Kaden turned the station to seventies music and turned the radio up to blast. I guess we were done talking relationship stuff, I chuckled to myself.

I liked people like Kaden, who say what they gotta say, then turn some good music on and be done with it. I'm sure if it hadn't been eight in the morning, we'd have had a beer to cap the whole conversation off.

To say I liked working in the shop with Kaden and his team was an understatement. I loved the smell of the wood, the sounds of the power tools, the loud music in the background.

Again, I think growing up on a farm and having similar days with my own dad and brother working in our tool shop had a significant impact on me. I truly hoped I could become more useful to Kaden over time because if I could talk him into taking me on as an apprentice, that would pretty much be the best life I could imagine.

Monday went as the others had before, me answering the million phone calls and trying to sweep around Kaden so he didn't have to walk on huge piles of sawdust. I also managed to continue sorting out some of the paperwork. There was a stack of invoices I found that caught my attention. Several of them seemed to be from various large companies around the area Kaden had done work for but that hadn't paid. I put those aside to ask Kaden about later.

To handle the phone calls a bit better, I put a new voice-mail message on Kaden's machine that told anyone who called that we were at least three months out from taking on any new business. I tried to answer as many calls as possible, but that was virtually impossible. Kaden was a popular carpenter and no wonder. His work was some of the best I'd ever seen.

I also understood why he didn't want to be filmed. If he actually did the Home Repair Network show, he'd have to hire a few personal assistants just to manage his phone.

During lunch, I plopped the invoices in front of Kaden and asked if he wanted me to check on them. He looked over at me and smiled.

"You remind me of Joseph's mom," he said. "She was in charge of the office and could sniff out an unpaid invoice like a fox could sniff out a rabbit. If you look in my documents, you'll see a form letter we send out as a reminder. These guys always pay, but they usually need a few reminders before they get around to it. I just haven't had time to chase them down."

"I'll be happy to do that," I said. "Did you hire anyone to handle the front office after your wife passed?"

"No, I thought I'd eventually just retire, so I didn't think I needed anyone," Kaden replied.

"Yeah," I said sarcastically. "I don't know how well you're doing on the retirement part of all this."

Kaden looked over and laughed. "I do seem to have missed the mark a bit."

"Are you really wanting to retire?" I asked.

Kaden thought for a moment. "To be honest, Daniel, I don't think I do. I like the work. I hate the phone and the paperwork, but I like being busy, and I like to play in my workshop."

We sat for a few moments eating our lunch before I said, "You know, I'm good at the paperwork stuff. In fact, I think I can get you pretty close to organized over the next three weeks that I'm here. That will give me something I can do while my arm heals. After that, I'd be very interested in working for you more like an apprentice. I'd love to be able to do some of the work you do. I'm far from an expert, but I've used power tools all my life and I'd love to learn."

Kaden considered it for a moment. "Let's have you hang out here for a while longer. This isn't the life for everyone. If, after the next three weeks, you're still interested, ask me again and we'll see where we are at that point."

I nodded and thanked him. That was about the best answer he could give, and I knew I was asking a lot. Training a new person to do something you did almost on autopilot was a lot of work, and I'd seen that the work, for Kaden, was almost like being in a meditative state.

Yeah, he had workers who came and went, but they were outside contractors who installed cabinets or vendors who brought products to the workshop. No one seemed to work with Kaden to design or build the pieces. The craftsmanship was something only he did, and we both knew that I was asking him to teach me.

Joseph picked me up at five on the dot. We headed to Beth's to fetch clothes and toiletries I'd need for the next day before grabbing a burger on the way through town toward Joseph's cabin.

"How tired are you?" Joseph asked.

"Not too tired, but my arm is a bit achy. Wanna go jump in the hot springs for a while?" I asked, only briefly thinking about the dream I'd had the night before.

"Uh-huh," Joseph smiled. "Race you there." And he took off like a jackrabbit. A warm feeling came over me. Even if Joseph hadn't warned me the night before, the dream certainly had, and

I knew tonight was going to be the night that Joseph and I took our relationship to the next level.

There was no way I was gonna keep up with those deliciously long legs, but I sprinted up the hill and down the trail toward where I thought the spring was.

Luckily, I guessed right, and when I saw Joseph, he was already in the pool. My heart skipped a beat as the memory of the dream hit me like a ton of bricks.

"Hope I don't turn into a freaking owl," I said quietly to myself.

Before I could strip down, I caught sight of Joseph's beautiful bronze, muscled body. Oh my God, I wanted my hands on him so bad. He was in the pool, sprawled out on the makeshift bench. He was grinning up toward me, and for some reason, tonight the water was so clear I could see every delicious part of that man's body glimmering in the pool. I quickly stripped and began to slip into the water.

"You seem happy to see me," he said and then looked down at my fully erect cock.

"You have no idea," I agreed, and I hissed as my foot went into the extremely hot water. "Damn, this water feels good." I'd been distracted by climbing into the pool, and when I stepped into the water, I immediately slipped into Joseph's waiting arms.

His hands slowly rose up my back and then down again. I wrapped my arms around his neck and allowed him to pull me into the deeper part of the pool. Our lips met in a sultry kiss that deepened into the promise of the things that were to come.

He pulled back and whispered in my ear. "I've wanted you for an awfully long time, Daniel. Now, I want to touch every part of you, lick every inch of you."

My breath caught at Joseph's words, and we pressed our bodies together, our cocks rubbing against one another as we continued to kiss.

Joseph's hands slid down my back and grasped my butt, thrusting me into his pelvis. He gently pushed me up against the side of the pool and moved his mouth to my neck, kissing and licking me, then moving down to my shoulders and my already hard nipples.

He lifted me slightly, so my waist was above water, took my cock into his mouth and began to move back and forth. The pleasure was exhilarating. I moaned as his tongue explored the head of my cock, then the shaft, and finally, he used his tongue to play with my balls before repeating the process.

"Joseph," I moaned. "God, your mouth feels so damned good."

He came back up to face me, his eyes looking into mine.

"You make me want to do things to your body that I've never done to any other person. Can I make love to you, Daniel?" he asked, his eyes fixed on mine.

The only thing I could do was plead. "Yes, Joseph. Please."

Joseph laid me back on the rock that jutted out from the water and lifted my legs into the air. His tongue explored the area between my balls and hole, nipping then licking, causing the nerves there to explode with electricity that made my whole body shiver. He put his hand on my cock, gently stroking it as his tongue slipped to my hole, moving across the sensitive muscles, making me moan his name. He thrust his tongue into the opening, then pulled out, before he assaulted my hole with his tongue again, each time the opening relaxed a bit more.

When he slipped me back into the water and sat me on the bench, he stayed underwater as he continued to stroke my cock. This time, he moved his finger into my hole, teasing it open.

"Joseph. Oh, God, Joseph, that feels so damned good." I moaned as he slipped his finger all the way in.

"You're so tight," he whispered, "I can't wait to fuck you."

I begged again. "Yes, please!"

Joseph had clearly thought ahead, and while kissing me, he reached over my shoulder and pulled a box toward him. When he opened the box, he pulled out a condom as well as a bottle of lube. He squeezed the lube onto his finger before reaching down and slipping two fingers in and out of me until my ass was utterly pliable.

"Fuck, me now, please, Joseph... I need you inside me."

"Soon enough," he whispered. "Be patient."

Patient? Fuck, I could only think about having him inside me. He thrust a third finger in, and I arched backward into the rock with a moan. I felt like I might melt into goo if he didn't fuck me soon. He put the condom on before lubing my ass and his cock.

"I want to watch you the first time I fuck you."

"God, Joseph," I groaned. "Do whatever you want, just get your cock inside me!"

Joseph chuckled and pushed his cock up against my opening, teasing me with his resistance.

"Are you sure you're ready?" Joseph asked.

Joseph's cock was certainly big and thick, but as I couldn't remember ever being this horny for someone in my life, there was probably no time in my life that I'd ever been *more* ready to be fucked.

"Damn, man, fuck me now!" I demanded.

I arched my back again as pleasure and pain mixed when he finally pushed his way into my hole. Slowly, he moved into me, and I felt the stretch around his huge cock as it assaulted my ass.

He noticed my grimace when the pain became intense and pulled back, but I put my legs around him and pulled him in toward me. After the initial pressure, my body relaxed, and he leaned down to kiss me. I continued pulling him toward my ass, and he didn't resist, giving me control over how much of him I took.

We never took our eyes off each other. He watched for the nuances of my ecstasy, making sure he didn't hurt me as he buried his massive dick deeper inside me. When he was finally all the way in, I looked at him and said, "Now, Joseph."

He laid his head down on mine. "I've never wanted anyone like I want you."

"Show me," I whispered.

He smiled, then stretched out one gloriously muscled arm and put his hand on my shoulder before moving that monster cock in and out of my ass, each stroke carrying me to a deeper level of sexual bliss.

After what felt like an eternity of him moving slowly in and out, he must've been confident I could handle all of him. He began to fuck me faster and faster until he was thrusting his cock all the way in and pounding me hard.

"God, yes, fuck yeah. Fuck me, baby, you feel so good inside me..."

I watched as the sweat beaded on his forehead and dripped down his face.

I was speechless, but I felt proud knowing he was that turned on by me.

My cries of ecstasy seemed to drive Joseph more and more over the edge.

His thrusts were magic, and I moaned in pure pleasure as he continued to pound into me, claiming me. Owning me.

When he leaned over and kissed me, never stopping his assault on my ass, I felt whole. Like a missing piece had finally been put back where it belonged.

When he shifted positions, I lifted up and said, "I want it doggy style. I wanna feel your balls slapping against my ass."

He grinned, and I turned over. When he entered me, his cock pushed against my prostate, and the pressure of that glorious dick touching my G-spot made me see stars.

He pulled out and then slowly began to move inside me again. "God, I'm gonna come. Fuck, you're hitting my... fuck..." I said, trying to tell him I wasn't going to last.

"I want you to come for me, Daniel," he moaned, and he began to stroke my cock, adjusting his thrusts so he was hitting square on my prostate. I exploded all over the rock in front of me.

Joseph arched against me and trembled as his own climax hit him.

He thrust into me again and again, as my cock finished pumping its load onto the rock. The final thrust forced the rest of my come out of me, and Joseph crumpled onto my back.

I slipped back into the water, and Joseph wrapped his arms around my body as he settled next to me. I put my head on his shoulder and snuggled into him.

"That was amazing," I said in a post-orgasmic daze.

He pulled away and looked at my face, presumably to see if I was joking.

"It'll get better," he said.

Something about the way he said that made me think he had some insight into our lovemaking that I was unaware of. Instead of questioning him, I just wanted to feel the emotional lightness that existed at that moment between us.

Before I knew it, the question was coming out of my mouth.

"Have you had sex here before?"

Then, thinking I didn't really want to know, I quickly said, "No, no, don't tell me."

Joseph laughed then pulled my face up so he could look me in the eyes.

"The answer to that is, no," Joseph said in a serious voice. "I've never brought a man to my home before, and I would never bring one here unless he was very special to me."

I didn't know how to respond. Tears stung the backs of my eyes with the feeling that it was something special. Not just sex but something... important.

The fact that he'd had the box sitting next to the pool made me think he could have possibly used this as a regular hook-up site.

"I'm glad you haven't," I answered honestly. "I want to think of this spot as our spot from now on." Then I snuggled back into his shoulder. Before long, Joseph slipped around and began to work my arm in the warm water again.

"Damn, I get the best fucking of my life and physical therapy all in one night," I joked.

"I just want you to get better," he said. "And besides, I like touching your arms and hands." Then he brought my hand up to his face and kissed my fingers one by one. The action caused my dick to wake back up, and I reached over with my other hand and let it rest on Joseph's face.

"You are a beautiful man, Joseph McCoy. I already want to make love to you again, and it hasn't even been thirty minutes since we last did it."

Joseph leaned back and laughed. "I thought you'd never ask."

We crawled out of the water and laid on a slab of rock away from the pool. As we allowed our bodies to cool off in the evening air, I climbed on top of Joseph. I let my cock rub his as I leaned over him, kissing him, then nibbling on his ear, then down to his throat, licking and sampling him as I went. His body was so perfectly proportioned, beautifully built biceps and triceps, each sitting atop a perfectly muscular arm. His shoulders were hard and strong, but when I put my head there, they seemed to cradle it perfectly. Somehow Joseph embodied the perfect hard muscular body, but with a softness you wouldn't expect on a man like him. I assumed it was because he built his muscles exploring the wilderness.

I allowed my tongue to travel down to his abdomen, where I traced his six-pack, moving across his stomach with my mouth, inhaling his forest scent.

Joseph's musky, forest aroma made me hunger for him like it was some magical elixir. I couldn't seem to get enough of the man. I wanted to touch, smell, and be touched by him all the time.

When my mouth got to his groin area, he was fully erect again. I explored his head, using my tongue to tease his slit while my lips wrapped around the edges where his head and shaft met. As I tasted each part of his beautiful cock, he moaned ever so slightly, and the sound sent shivers down my back and into my own cock. I grasped his balls in my hand and gently allowed my mouth to move up and down his shaft. When I finally took his entire girth into my mouth, Joseph arched and moaned under me. I was sure at that point that if I hadn't just come a few minutes earlier, the sound of him receiving pleasure from me would have caused me to come right then and there.

I put my mouth over his cock, moving slowly, then I picked up pressure and speed. My finger explored his butt, then slowly, as I moved faster, I let that finger find his hole and began to tease his guardian muscle.

Before I knew it, Joseph put his hands in my hair and groaned loudly like he was about to come again. I thrust my finger into his hole until I found his prostate and massaged as I sucked him.

"Oh, God, Daniel. Oh, God!"

Cum exploded into my mouth. I swallowed it and moved up just as Joseph sat up and took my mouth with his.

"One second earlier, and you would've had a snowball," I teased. He smiled and licked my lips.

"Nothing is hotter than tasting myself on your tongue."

I cocked my eyebrow at him and licked his lips before saying, "Mmm, I'll remember that for next time."

Joseph rolled me over and lay on top of me, kissing me while his beautiful body pressed mine into the slab of granite underneath us.

"Are you ready to go back to the cabin?" he finally asked me.

"Can we have more sex there?" I asked.

He snickered and said, "If you give me a minute, maybe we can have a lot more sex there."

"Then, by all means," I said lazily. "Lead the way."

We made love all through the night and into the next morn-ing. I wasn't sure how I was going to manage work the next day, but I made a point of not thinking about that since it was Joseph's dad I worked for.

Eleven

F or some reason, I had no difficulty staying awake for the workday. I heard myself humming along with the music and was in a better mood than I'd been in weeks. I could tell Kaden had noticed, but he didn't say anything.

I was more than pleased because, for the life of me, I couldn't imagine what I would tell him if he asked. Despite my post-sex euphoric haze, by the late afternoon, the lack of sleep began to catch up with me. Kaden came in around three-thirty and announced we were done for the day.

"I'll run you back over to Beth's," he said. "Then I'm going to go run some errands."

Maybe because my mind was full of my own happy love thoughts, I smiled at Kaden and asked, "Those errands involve a nurse by chance?"

Kaden turned narrowed eyes at me and simply said, "I haven't asked you why you're so happy today, and you don't ask me about nurses."

I couldn't help but laugh out loud, and putting my hand up in the air, I said, "I won't ask but tell Sam I said hi."

Kaden walked out but not before I heard him say something about "little shit." I looked up and noticed before he turned the corner, there was a smile on his face.

Beth wasn't home, so I went up to my room and fell asleep on the bed. Several hours later, I had the most luxurious dream of Joseph's beautiful body wrapping itself around me. I woke to find him curled up in my bed spooning me.

Damn, if I didn't like waking up that way. I rolled over to face him and he slowly opened sleepy eyes. "Aunt B sent me up an hour ago to wake you and see what you wanted for dinner. I disobeyed her and decided I'd rather fall asleep with you instead."

"Mmm," I moaned happily. "I'm glad you did. I'm worried about Beth skinning you alive, but it was worth it to wake up in your arms."

Joseph leaned over and kissed me. "So, what do you want for dinner?" he asked.

"Let me think," I said and stretched, letting my good hand slip up his thighs and grasp his already growing cock.

"We better save that for later," Joseph said. "I doubt Aunt B will tolerate much hanky-panky before she gets dinner served."

"You're probably right," I said.

We got up, wandered downstairs and found Beth sitting in front of a large pizza. "I figured you boys were busy, so I just ordered a pizza. Help yourself," she said.

I went over and kissed her on the cheek. "Thanks for taking care of us," I said.

She looked at me and winked. "When you're in the throes of love, it helps to have someone to make sure there's sustenance. I'm guessing you'll both be needing all the energy you can get."

Neither Joseph nor I made eye contact or looked at Beth. There was no way to manage the conversation without it becoming seriously uncomfortable.

Beth just laughed at us. "Like the whole world can't tell the two of you finally hooked up. Well, it is about time, now all that teenage angst the two of you have been emitting can finally be given back to the teenagers it belongs to!" She laughed and stood up. "What will you boys be having to drink? I've got beer or water, you choose."

We both took a beer, and since it was clear Beth knew everything, we sat as close to each other as possible while we ate. Beth talked about the new book she'd started and told us it was going to be a great one. As promised, the characters were based loosely on us, but she said they had sex way before the two of us got around to it.

"Aunt B, do all your characters run around having sex like rabbits?" Joseph asked.

Beth looked at him and shrugged. "Have you ever read a romance novel? That's the entire point of the book, honey. Two people hooking up and falling in love. I found it's best to get the sex out of the way so the characters can focus on the falling in love part." Then she winked at Joseph and looked over at me but didn't say any more than that.

Joseph didn't spend the night that night, saying he had a ridiculously early job the next morning. There was a mating pair of bald eagles he needed to see and document, and if he wanted to see their eaglets, he had to get up before sunrise. The eaglets tended to be more active just after sunup and he wanted to get a few good pictures of them to document on the park website.

When he left, I felt lonely. How was it just a few weeks had passed, and I already missed the guy when he was gone less than a couple minutes? Beth saw my expression before I could hide it, and she just shook her head.

"You boys have both got it bad," she said. "That is both a good and a bad thing." She came over and put her hand on my shoulder. "The best affairs can burn hot in the beginning but burn themselves out. The relationships that last the longest tend to be the ones that simmer, burn hot, then simmer again. Don't be in too big a hurry with this one, Daniel. Let the heat burn low and strong. I tell you now that boy needs space, and even though he'll want you all the time, he needs to be without you while his heart is building those bonds."

"It isn't like we have a choice, Mrs. Beth," I sighed. "His work is solitary, and he needs to be out in the wilderness. I would never want to take him away from that, but that doesn't mean I won't miss him while he's gone."

"No, honey," she said. "To love Joseph means you will spend many days of your life alone. It is good you know that going in. Besides, don't they say, *absence makes the heart grow fonder?*"

I smiled at her but thought to myself, *I'm not so clingy that I can't give a man space.* I wasn't sure why his family thought I couldn't. Were they trying to warn me he needed solitude, or were they assuming I couldn't give him space? Oh well, it wasn't worth being concerned about. I hugged Beth, said good night, and went back to bed.

I lay awake, thinking about Joseph's and my personalities. Joseph's family were quick to suggest how to be with Joseph or that he needed space. I wondered if maybe I was missing something. How much space did he need? Was I clinging onto him and not realizing it? It seemed to me that Joseph was pursuing me, but I knew I could be overwhelming, even clingy when I started seeing someone.

I woke up an hour before my phone went off, wandered down to the empty kitchen, and put on a pot of coffee. I sat staring at nothing, thinking about Joseph, me and all the stuff that had led me to where I was. I had begun to feel like I belonged in Port Angeles.

Strangely, that was really the first time I'd ever felt that way. Was I about to jeopardize it by dating the town sweetheart? I knew without a doubt that I would fall in love with Joseph, given enough time. My heart was already leaning that way, and in a way, it had never done that with any other guy I'd dated.

Also, he was a hero. Not only did he help drag me off the mountain, but he was nice and sweet about it afterward. He ensured I got to a safe place after the hospital, and he put me in the care of Beth. Now, Beth was a lifelong friend, something else I knew innately.

Joseph was the real deal. The whole package and although they all seemed to accept what was happening between him and me, there was a constant warning that I could hurt him, or he would lose himself by being with me. There was nothing I wanted less than that. Why would anyone clip the feathers of a beautiful bird? Wasn't it more rewarding to watch that bird fly?

By the time Kaden showed up for me, I'd convinced myself I needed to give Joseph more space. He didn't need a clingy Southern belle keeping him from enjoying the life he loved. I'd rather cut my arm off than cause him to lose that. It was what made him who he was. I was going to begin putting the walls back up starting that night and not just with him but with all of them. Maybe if I could keep everyone at a distance, I would still belong here after these weeks were over.

Kaden kept me running all day. Not only did the phone ring nonstop, but Kaden wanted my help every few minutes holding plywood, or a two-by-four, as he cut and put them into place. I was glad I put the message on the phone because Kaden seemed to be testing my resolve for the apprenticeship. Well, I'd be damned if he didn't leave that day being impressed. *Give me what you got, Kaden. Let me show you my resolve.*

That night, I needed more painkillers. I decided to call the doc the next day and make sure I wasn't pushing too hard. I didn't want to let Kaden down, but I also didn't want to push the healing process back either. In the end, if Kaden was going to offer it, I wanted to ensure I would be in top form for the apprenticeship.

Joseph called late that night, but I ignored the call. Of course, I wanted nothing more than to talk to him, but if he needed space, then I'd be damned if he didn't get it from me.

The rest of the week was like Tuesday. I worked my ass off with Kaden challenging me a little more each day. The doc said if I didn't strain or put the arm in a compromising position, including not lifting heavy objects, I should be okay.

Despite that, I ended up taking a lot of Ibuprofen that week. Damn, I was ready for the weekend when it came. Friday, Kaden took me back to Beth's, and before he dropped me off, asked, "So, you still think you're up to the job?"

I smiled at Kaden and winked. "You haven't scared me off yet, old man," I replied, and he laughed.

"I'll do a better job next week," he replied, returning my wink. "I was going easy on you because of the arm."

Despite my inner voice screaming in my head, I just smiled back and said, "Bring it on."

I turned to go into the house and caught sight of Joseph standing in the doorway. Damn, that man made my legs wobbly. "Aren't you a sight for sore eyes..." Inwardly, I sighed, thinking I had more sore feet if I were being accurate.

"You got a minute?" he asked.

"For you, I have two," I said smiling. Joseph didn't return my smile. "What's going on?"

Joseph turned on me. "You tell me. I've been calling you all week, and you haven't answered or returned my calls. The least you could've done was text me."

"I was giving you space," I said sheepishly.

"Who asked you to give me space?" he asked his voice getting louder. I looked around Beth's neighborhood and thought I needed to try to take this inside before we put on a show for the neighbors.

"Come on in, Joseph," I said. "I just got home. I'll explain."

"Goddamnit, Daniel, I don't need your explanations. You and I made love. I touched you, and you touched me. In a way I've never done with another human being on the fucking planet, and then you *fall off* the damned planet, leaving me in the dust like you don't give a fucking shit!"

All I could do was stand there like a dummy with my mouth open. I could only imagine I looked like one of the hillbillies who sat in their yards, in front of their forty-year-old trailer houses surrounded by garbage. When I finally got my wits about me, I felt some of the anger Joseph was spewing at me.

"Well, then you need to have a fucking talk with your family because every damned one of them told me to leave you the hell alone, that you need space, that I'm smothering the fuck out of you. What do you want from me? All I want to do is jump you, kiss you, make love to you, but I don't want to hold you back, either. I don't want to be the reason you can't go do what you love, so I gave you some damned space."

I turned to go into the house, and Joseph stopped me. "Wait, who told you to give me space?"

"Everyone. Everyone who knows you told me to give you space. Like I'm smothering you or some goddamned thing. Joseph," I said, defeated, "I'm exhausted. Your dad has run me through the mill, not that I would have it any other way. But right now, I have no interest in standing out here and putting on a show with you for all the damned neighbors."

I walked into the house and slammed the door behind me. Beth was looking at me with her eyes the size of saucers. I looked back at her and just moaned. "I don't think I'll need anything to eat tonight, Mrs. Beth," I said and went upstairs.

I laid in bed for a while trying to calm down, but the longer I stayed there, the angrier I got. I sat up and tried playing a game on the computer, but after my poor avatar got clobbered for the umpteenth time, I decided to give that up as well.

I threw some jogging pants on and headed out to get a run in. I didn't see Beth on my way out and didn't need to explain to anyone why I was angry or hear why the man I was obsessed with needed space again.

I ran out along one of the back alleys thinking the thing I could use the most about then was to smell the sea and feel the cool breeze as I processed how the fuck I'd screwed up trying to fix whatever I'd screwed up before.

As I ran, I could feel the anger flowing from me into the ground with each pound of my foot on the pavement. Exercise was always my best defense against intense emotions. At least running along a public highway, I was unlikely to fall off a mountain like I had before. I was trying to figure out what I was going to do, whether or not I should go back to Seattle and leave the whole thing behind. I wasn't really paying attention to the traffic, and before I knew it, a car had come up behind me. When I finally heard the car, it was too late. The idiot driver must have been drunk because he clipped me, and I spun off the road, into a pole.

"Fucking H. Christ!" I yelled. Luckily, an older couple was following behind the car, saw me get clipped, and pulled over to check on me.

"Son, are you okay?" the lady asked.

"Um..." I stammered. "I'm not sure. Give me a minute." I stood up, but my head was spinning where I'd rammed it into the damned pole.

I gripped the pole for a moment and waited for the world to stop moving.

"Maybe a little worse for wear," I replied. The older man had gotten out of the passenger side and led me to the back seat. He'd pulled a first aid kit out from somewhere and was mopping my face.

"Did you guys happen to get that guy's license plate?" I asked. They both shook their heads.

"No, we were just coming home from a late dinner and saw the car pull out as we were coming toward you. He must have been drunk because it looked like he actually sped up when he saw you."

"Well, shit," I said, then looked at the couple and apologized. "I'm sorry about the language."

The couple laughed. "That language doesn't bother us," the old man replied with a chuckle. He took off the bloody gauze and said, "You are going to have to have stitches, I'm afraid. We'll run you over to the hospital."

"Are you sure?" I asked miserably. "I kinda hate hospitals."

The old man laughed and said he did too, especially since he'd been an ER doc for over fifty years.

"In that case, I'll take your word on the stitches thing, and thanks," I replied.

The couple took me to the hospital and introduced me to the front desk staff, who checked me in. As soon as that was done, the old doctor took me back to where a nurse was sitting. He explained what happened and then left me in her hands. After she'd taken more information, she finished cleaning the wound and told me to hold a fresh gauze on it.

"Don't be alarmed," she said, "but head wounds bleed a lot. Keep that gauze on there, or you'll be covered from head to toe before I get back."

I assured her I would. Within a few minutes, a sheriff's deputy showed up and asked me questions about the incident. I told him what I remembered, which wasn't much since I'd only seen the son of a bitch seconds before he mowed me down.

"Do you think this has anything to do with the incidents that occurred in Seattle?" he asked.

I looked at him in shock for a moment. "You already know about that?"

"Yeah, when Doc Barnes called, I pulled your record up. The police in Edmonds let us know that you'd been robbed, and someone was trying to follow you."

I nodded but immediately regretted it. "Yeah, I have an ex-friend who we think broke in, ripped my clothing up and trashed my room. He also probably hired the private detective who was following me. But," I thought for a moment, "this isn't something he'd do. He's too chicken shit for all that. No, I think this was just a random drunk who tagged me and then drove off."

The deputy nodded and said that, regardless, he'd let the Edmonds detectives know about it just in case they were linked in any way.

I thanked him, and he turned to leave. "Oh," he said. "Joseph McCoy is outside in the waiting room. I called Mrs. Clemens to let her know you'd been hit. I'm guessing she sent Joseph to come pick you up."

Then he chuckled and said, "Good luck with that. I'm guessing Annabeth is mad enough to kill. I sure wouldn't want to be your drunk driver about now."

"No, she isn't gonna be too happy with me about now either," I said, mistakenly shaking my head before once again regretting it.

The doctor came in right after the deputy left. She smiled a huge smile and introduced herself as Dr. Elizabeth Barnes.

"As in the old Dr. Barnes that brought me in?" I asked.

"That would be the one. He's my father-in-law," she said cheerfully.

I chuckled to myself. "Small towns," I said, and she agreed as she stitched up my wound.

"They'll need to stay in for a week, then you need to come back and have them removed. Also, my in-laws want you and Joseph to come by tomorrow so they can check on you. They said they'd come to you, but until they catch the guy who hit you, they're afraid of getting on Annabeth's bad side."

"Oh, Lord, does that woman really rule the town that much?" I asked.

"If you know Annabeth, you already know the answer to that," the doctor chuckled. "Joseph knows where my in-laws live. Meanwhile, you need to get plenty of rest. I'd like someone to check up on you throughout the night. Otherwise, sleep is what you need."

"Aren't I supposed to stay awake for a while after a concussion?"

"No," she said. "That's an old recommendation. Now we know that someone with a concussion needs to get a lot of rest to heal. You'll have a nasty headache tonight and probably tomorrow. Just take Tylenol to manage the pain and if anything changes, check back with me or your regular doctor. Now, as for the in-laws, do visit them if you can, they were really worried about you."

I managed to agree without making the mistake of nodding or moving my head again.

My head was pounding when they finally wheeled me out into the waiting room. Joseph jumped up when he saw me and came over before they could wheel me outside.

"Daniel, I'm…"

I put my hand up and said, "You're absolutely right to be angry. I'm fucking this up, not you, and this stupid bump on the head has nothing to do with you and everything to do with me not paying attention. Again!" I said in frustration. "Now, if you don't mind, let's save the arguing until tomorrow. My head feels like it could split in half."

I noticed the nurse look at Joseph in a meaningful way, but my head hurt too badly to try to interpret what it meant. When Joseph had me tucked into the front seat of the car, he ran around to the driver's side and climbed in.

"I've decided to go back to Edmonds tomorrow," I said. "This is too much to put on you or Beth. Hell, it's too much to put on any of you." Before I could help myself, a tear slipped out.

"The hell you will," Joseph said under his breath. Then he turned to me. "You will stay at Aunt B's because that's what was agreed to. Daniel, you have a whole group of people who care and are worried about you, and you are not going to run away from us because you're embarrassed or upset. Besides, according to Dr. and Mrs. Barnes, it isn't you that should be embarrassed, it's the drunken fool who struck you and ran away like a damned coward."

Completely done in, I leaned my head against the back of the seat, and in the darkness, let the tears stream. I just hoped it was dark enough that Joseph wasn't able to tell I was crying.

When I went into the house, Beth, Martha, Kaden, and Sam were all sitting around the living room. Beth jumped up when she saw us and put me squarely in the high back recliner, pulled my feet up, and put a cold, wet towel on my forehead.

"We've been told by the doc that you need to get plenty of rest, but before you do, we've got something to say. There's not even a need for you to say anything, we'll do all the talking." Then she turned to the group and looked at each of them pointedly before looking back at me. They all nodded.

"Guys, before you lecture me, please understand, I have a splitting headache. I know I'm an idiot, and I really don't think I have it in me to be dressed down for my inadequacies. If you don't mind, I'd rather just go to my room."

"No one here is going to dress you down. In fact, we are the ones who'll be doing all the apologizing tonight," Beth said. "I'll start. Joseph, you sit down over there because this involves you as well."

Beth took a deep breath and began. "Joseph is my only nephew, and we are all a little too attached to him. I'm the first to say I'm overprotective of him. Not everyone in Joseph's life has been kind or understanding of him. He's had his share of people who pretended to be his friends but turned out to be better described as enemies."

I turned a surprised look at Joseph to see him squirming and very uncomfortable with the conversation.

"Because of this, I think all of us have been guilty of trying to direct how the two of you have been getting on. Unfortunately, our interfering has created nothing but a chaotic mess. Even though we told you Joseph needed space, what we were trying to say is that he is amazing, beautiful, and a great catch just like he is. We didn't want anyone to try to change him."

Beth sat down, and Kaden looked over at me and said, "We needed to butt out of this and let you and Joseph do it on your own, however you need to do it. Parents and overprotective aunts shouldn't be interfering with brand new relationships. So, the three of us have made a pact. From now on, we are going to butt out."

Joseph burst out laughing when his dad finished. "Yeah, right, like that'll ever happen," he said.

His dad gave him the eye, but before he could stop himself, he laughed. "Okay, we promise to try to butt out. How's that?"

"More realistic," Joseph said. "But still a stretch."

"What my family isn't telling you, Daniel, is that I've had my heart stomped on more than once. I've run up against some pretty significant losers. The last one tried to force me to move to the city with him, and when I didn't come running, he gave me an ultimatum. That was tough, especially since Mom was sick at the time, and being back in Seattle made the most sense. But I couldn't, wouldn't leave, so *he* left me."

Joseph looked around at his family. "What my family has neglected to see is that I'm not a young lovesick teenager any longer," he said. "I was only nineteen when that went down. The guy was a jackass when I met him. He was trying to find someone he could mold. That was never going to be me, and it isn't fair to compare Daniel to the likes of him."

Joseph came over to kneel beside me on the floor. "My family are overwhelming and way too involved at times, but I think it's because we all like you so much." Before I could help it, the tears began to flow again.

"You all realize this is really unfair, I have a headache and you're being sweet. There's no way I can be held accountable for any emotional outbursts that are likely to occur."

The group laughed, and one by one, they came over and either hugged me, put a hand on mine, or in the case of Beth, kissed my cheek. By the time they were done, the room was empty except for Joseph, across from me, still kneeling on the floor.

"I'm sorry about my crazy family," he said. "I should have known they would interfere with this one way or another." He waited a moment, then moved closer and took my hand. "I wasn't just angry earlier, I was hurt. I have never been with anyone like I was with you. When you didn't return my calls or texts, I went a little bit off the deep end. Believe it or not, I was even jealous of Aunt B and Dad for having all that time with you while I was stuck in the woods working."

Despite the pain, I laughed. "So, while I was doing everything I could think of to take my mind off you, trying to give you space, you were spending all your time upset because I wasn't more clingy?"

"Apparently," Joseph laughed.

"Okay, so, let's make a deal. When you need space, you tell me you need space. Otherwise, I'll just be myself and love on you as much as you'll let me. Deal?" I asked.

"That sounds like a great deal," he said with a sigh. "Now, about why you got hit."

"Oh, let's not talk about that now."

He put his hands up in surrender. "That's fine," Joseph said, "but we need to talk about it soon. We're all concerned this could be connected to what happened in Seattle and the asshole who's out to get you."

"This wasn't Nathan. He's underhanded and sneaky, but he's a total coward. He's a stab you in the back kind of guy, not run you over with a car. No, like I told the deputy at the hospital, I wasn't paying attention and some drunk dude clipped me as he drove by."

"That may be the case, but to be safe, I want you to stay close to one of us from now on, at least until the cops find out who hit you. It's a small town, and I'm sure someone saw something. People don't miss much around here." Joseph sat back on his heels. "Speaking of that, I'm sorry about the breakdown in the front yard. You were right, I knew all the neighbors were watching, but all I could think was that you weren't really that interested in me, and like I said, I went a little nuts.

"Daniel, before we go much further, I do need to ask you, are you sure you want to keep going? I'm getting attached maybe a bit too fast, and if you want to end this, we should probably do it now while there's something left of me to salvage."

I sighed, reached over, and grabbed Joseph's hand.

"I'm always the one who moves too fast. With you, I keep trying to slow things down because I've never wanted something to work as much as this. I like you too much, and that's a truth I probably shouldn't tell you, but there it is. I don't care if you need space, or if you need to spend a week in the woods, or if you need to hump my ass every night, I want to keep working this out with you and see where it goes."

Joseph smiled, leaned over and kissed me. "So, should we let my family off the hook? You know they're all standing in the kitchen waiting on us to forgive them."

I laughed at that and yelled despite the pain. "Okay, you are all forgiven. You can come back in."

Of course, they were waiting to hear that, and soon they were all back in the living room, and our conversations returned to their normal round of topics. When I finally began to drift off, Sam came over and checked my pupils.

"You seem to be doing fine," she said. "Get lots of rest tonight and tomorrow." She gestured for Joseph to come help me to my room.

I got up, still a little wobbly, which was embarrassing in front of a room full of people, but Joseph's strong arms kept me stable. He put his arm around my waist and guided me toward the stairs. "You just want to touch my butt," I teased and heard several snickers behind me.

"I admit *nothing*," Joseph said with his own snicker.

When we got to the room, he started taking my clothes off. I laughed. "If you think I'd be able to get it up tonight, you might be overestimating my ability to perform."

"Um, no," Joseph laughed. "I'm just trying to get you into bed."

"Isn't that what I said?" I teased.

"After being without you for a whole week, I can't deny I'd love to jump your bones, but I'd rather those bones be ready for a jumping when I do."

I leaned over to him, which made my head start to pound and I winced.

"If I didn't feel like shit, I'd be begging you to jump these bones," I said, "but you better just hold off a day or two, especially now that I know you don't really want all that space. Hopefully, we can have a lot more sex!"

Joseph grinned and pulled my shirt off, which he'd managed to unbutton while I flirted with him. I pulled my own pants off and was crawling into bed when he crawled in next to me. I turned around, surprised.

"You're going to stay with me?" I asked.

"Of course, I am," he said. "Doc told me you need someone to keep an eye on you throughout the night, and I've been daydreaming about all the different ways I can do that."

"You slut," I chuckled, and Joseph belted out a laugh. "God, I'm so happy you're staying. I've missed you so much, my body is desperate to feel you touch it. Even if there is no sex."

"Sex will come later," he promised. "For now, just rest."

Joseph's beautiful body folded perfectly around me, and I fell asleep with my head resting on his bicep. I would never get used to how wonderful it was to fall asleep engulfed in the aroma of Joseph's musky forest smell.

I dreamed of being a snowy owl flying through the forest, running free and wild with the wind blowing through my wings. As the glee filled me, something shifted and a car swerved behind me, clipping me and breaking my wing. As I fell to the ground, I heard laughter, evil laughter, and I woke up gasping for air. Joseph was right there with his arms tightly around me and his soothing voice telling me he was there, that he had me, I was safe. I fell back asleep almost immediately, and there were no more dreams of flying or evil drunken drivers.

The next day, I woke up with what had to be the worst hangover I'd ever had. When Joseph asked me how I felt, I admitted, "I haven't hurt this much since the day after I got into Uncle Cleo's shine jug when I was nine years old."

"You do come from colorful people," Joseph snickered.

"You truly have no idea," I replied. "One day, we'll go there, and you can see for yourself."

Joseph snuggled up to me. "I'm afraid."

"You should be," I said. "You *really* should be!"

Joseph reached over to my side of the bed and opened a bottle of Tylenol and had a glass of water waiting for me.

"When did you do this?" I asked.

"I woke up to check on you a few times during the night, and I slipped downstairs and grabbed this knowing you'd need it when you woke up."

"Bless you," I said. "When this hits, I'd be willing to sell my soul to the devil to get some coffee."

"I doubt you'll have to do that," Joseph answered. "Aunt B will give you coffee for free, no soul required."

I loved how Joseph made me laugh even when my head felt like it had grown fifteen sizes larger and was banging onto the sides of the bedroom.

"Thank you for staying with me last night," I said. "It felt so awesome to wake up in your arms this morning, despite the headache or maybe because of it." Joseph cuddled in and kissed my neck, giving me chill bumps that spread throughout my body.

"It was selfish. I really just wanted... no, needed to hold you again, and since you were hurt, I couldn't do anything else. Besides, I got to look like a hero to my family... and to you," he teased.

"You are my hero, Joseph," I said. "You have been since the minute I met you."

I turned over, morning breath and all, and kissed him squarely on the mouth. He kissed me back before I accidentally told him I loved him. I'd come to that conclusion during the previous evening's discussion, but there was no need for me to tell him all that right now.

We got up, and I balanced my head long enough to get to the kitchen and begin plying my system with coffee. As the Tylenol and the caffeine began to take hold, my forty-foot head began to shrink back down to a more normal size.

"I am such a caffeine addict," I admitted. "I didn't use to be this bad, but something about this part of the world turns you into either a user or a pusher or both."

Both Beth and Joseph agreed. "It isn't like you can't literally go onto almost any street corner in any town in the Pacific Northwest and buy an espresso," Joseph admitted.

"Thank God," I sighed.

"Do you feel like riding over to visit Doc and Mrs. Barnes?" Beth asked. "They've already called once last night and again this morning to check on you. They seem to be rather taken with you, Daniel."

Then she smiled. "I asked them why they didn't want to come over here, and Doc Barnes admitted that he was afraid I blamed them for the accident. I guess the whole town already knows you're one of mine." Then she chuckled and made herself busy around the kitchen.

Funny thing was, I kinda thought of myself as one of hers too. It's so funny how, when you find your people, you seem to fit right in without even trying. I went over to where Beth was washing the coffee cups in the sink and hugged her from behind.

"Thanks for letting me be one of yours," I said. "I needed that more than you know."

Beth turned around, and I saw she had tears in her eyes. "I'm such a ninny," she said. "I've always been such a damned fag hag, and I admit, I've fallen in love with you."

She kissed my cheek, then wiped her eyes. "I won't lie and say I wasn't scared out of my wits last night when the deputy called and said you'd been hit. All I could think of was this was my fault for all that crap I told you about Joseph. When I found out you were okay, I called the whole family in and lectured them, including myself, for being so damned over-protective of Joseph, we forgot to protect you. That won't be happening again, and that is a promise," she said.

"I am so happy you love Joseph enough to be overprotec-tive. In your shoes, I'd be the exact same way," I admitted. "That's what family is all about."

I reached over and kissed Joseph on the mouth, then said, "And this one is lucky to have all of you."

"I think we are lucky to have found you too," Joseph said before kissing me back.

I leaned back from the kiss and looked over at Beth, who was still wiping her eyes. "Okay," I said. "That is enough mushy for all of us. I'm going back to my room and having a shower, then we can go over to the Doc's and ease their worry."

Then I turned around and smiled a mischievous smile. "Wanna go with us, Mrs. Beth?"

She chuckled. "I'll be ready in a few minutes."

I couldn't wait to see the old man's face when we showed up with the very personification of his fears. I would have to get to the bottom of why he, of all people, was afraid of little Annabeth Clemens. That had to be a good story.

Doc and Mrs. Barnes were a sweet couple who lived in one of the nicely landscaped older homes down by the old town center. They were sitting on their front porch when we arrived and invited us to join them there.

Mrs. Barnes ran in and brought out lemonade for each of us and then sat down next to me. They had several questions about what had happened the night before. I could tell they were trying to remember as much as possible, but unfortunately, none of us had much recollection of who was driving the car and not much more information about the car itself.

Eventually, the conversation turned to the goings-on around the Port Angeles area. Beth and the Doc were full of gossip, and Mrs. Barnes just sat across from them and smiled as they talked about the different people around town – Mr. Jones was adding on to his garage, Mrs. Smith had decided not to sell tomatoes, Farmer Joe was thinking about selling the lavender farm, and so forth and so on. As their conversation continued, my mind wandered to what it must be like to know each person who lived around you so well you were aware when one of them decided not to plant enough tomatoes to sell.

Growing up in a small town meant my parents had that kind of relationship with their neighbors, but somehow, it was different for me. I left when I was seventeen. I graduated two months before my eighteenth birthday and headed straight for Seattle.

My parents had been killed the year before, and Paul told me that as soon as I was done with school, I was welcome to join him and Jeff there. I didn't think I'd even thought about there being another alternative. As a result, the time when my classmates had begun building adult relationships in the community didn't happen for me. My adult years had started in the big city, and I didn't really know much about the people around me. Hearing Beth and the Barnes' talk and Joseph's occasional reply made me realize how much I missed living in a small town. I wanted to know the people around me, and I wanted to care about their annual summer crop of tomatoes or if someone was adding on to their garage.

Joseph must have noticed my mind had wandered, and he leaned over and asked me if I was okay. I smiled at him, once again struck by how wonderful this man seemed to be, ever vigilant of the people around him.

"I'm okay," I said, then reached over and took his hand. "I'm just thinking about how nice it is to sit on a front porch and discuss the events of a small community. I admit I miss it." Joseph smiled back at me.

Doc Barnes had noticed our conversation and asked how my head was feeling.

"I'm better," I assured him. "Just a low throb now, not in pain like it was earlier."

"You'll need to rest as much as possible and not overdo it for a couple days," he said. "Concussions are nasty things, and if not properly healed, can cause some serious damage."

"I'm just happy you two were there last night and found me so quickly after the accident. I doubt I'd have been much good on my own, and I can't imagine a lot of people would've been very keen on stopping to help a stranger covered in blood."

They smiled and said they were glad to help but didn't contradict the stranger covered in blood part.

We left soon after, with me using the excuse that I'd need more Tylenol soon and could use a nap, which was honest enough. Although my headache was better, I was still pretty tired and when we got back to Beth's, I went upstairs for that nap. Joseph followed me up, and I kissed him and let him know if he needed to get something done, I was going to be pretty useless for the rest of the day. He told me he needed to catch up on some paperwork, and we both agreed to meet Sunday afternoon for lunch.

When he kissed me, he took my face in his hands and said, "One day, I want you to be at my home so I can take care of you. Maybe, after this week, you'll agree to come stay with me."

"I don't know, Joseph, that's a big step, and I can be a lot to deal with. Heck, I can't even go for a run without getting hit by a car."

Joseph smiled. "It's because you are so handsome. The driver must have been temporarily stunned by your beauty."

"Yeah," I chuckled. "I'm sure that's exactly what happened."

We kissed again before he left. I admit, when he was gone, my heart really missed him. I wasn't sure it was a good idea for us to stay together, though. I decided that I'd run it by Beth and get her opinion. She had a way of breaking things down, and after last night's apology, I was sure she'd be honest with me.

Before I laid down, I gave Paul a call. I'd been avoiding it, not because I wanted to keep him at arm's length like I'd done before, but because I knew when he heard about the accident, he'd be worried. But I'd made a promise not to leave him out of the loop any longer and it was time to make good on that promise.

I called Paul's mobile. He didn't answer, so I left a message. "Hey, Paul. I just wanted you to know last night I was jogging and a car tapped me. I jumped out of the car's way and bumped my head on a pole. Anyway, I just wanted you to know and don't worry, I have a couple stitches, but I'm good. I'm going to take a nap now but feel free to give me a call back if you want more information." I disconnected and lay down. Once again, I was asleep before my head hit the pillow.

I woke up around four-thirty and could hear voices downstairs. I popped a couple more Tylenol, went to the bathroom and brushed my teeth, then headed downstairs. I was more than a little shocked to find my brother and Jeff sitting at Beth's kitchen island.

"Hey guys," I said as I came into the kitchen. "What are you doing here?"

Paul looked over and said, "Well, we heard you got hit by a car and decided that was worth a visit."

"I'm sorry," I sighed, "I didn't mean to scare you. It was a tap really, and mostly my fault. I was running and not paying much attention. I think the driver must have been drunk or something because he'd swerved onto my side of the road. Anyway, I'm good, see." And I moved my hands to indicate I was still standing.

"It is the 'or something' that we're concerned about," Paul said.

Paul, Jeff, and I hugged, then I sat down across the island from them.

"So, I spoke to one of the deputies this morning. They don't think this has anything to do with Nathan or Tony. Besides, Nathan is a coward, and Tony will have forgotten I ever existed by now. There really weren't that many brain cells up there to retain much information." I chuckled, but Paul didn't see the humor. "Paul, seriously, you can't think Nathan would be brave enough to try to hit me with a car. Besides, why would he even want to do that? As far as he is concerned, he's gonna get me through the court system. He's such a narcissistic idiot that he thinks he can't lose."

"I don't know," Paul admitted, "but I don't trust anyone who'd break into someone's house and mutilate their clothing."

"According to the police, he has a pretty reliable alibi for that night. He and Tony were breaking up publicly at some restaurant downtown. Apparently, it was pretty serious. God, I'd have given big money to have been a fly on that wall." Again, I laughed, but Paul didn't. "Brother, you have to lighten up. There is no conspiracy here. I wasn't paying attention and some drunk dude barely tapped me."

"So, who broke into our house and ripped up your clothes?" Paul asked.

"My best guess is it was some homeless queen Nathan hired to scare me. He would do crap like that all the time. I'm guessing he's shitting himself right now, scared that he's gonna get in trouble with the law." I walked over and put my hand on my brother's shoulder. "Thank you for being worried, but I'm fine. There is no one out there that could possibly want me dead enough to go to the effort of killing me."

Then I smiled a crooked smile at Paul. "With the exception of you, of course."

Paul moved, and before I could dodge him, he literally kicked my butt. "And don't you forget it either!" he said.

Sensing the mood had shifted, Beth came into the kitchen and asked what everyone would like for dinner. "Let's go out," I said. "Paul's treat." He tried to kick me again, but I was prepared and darted to the other side of the island.

"It would be my treat, Mrs. Beth. Where would you like to go eat tonight?" She pondered a moment, and after we debated over a few places, we all decided to try a new Thai place that had just opened a few months ago.

"I've been told the food is good," Beth replied. "But haven't had a date to go try it out. This way, I can be on the arm of three good-looking men." Then she chuckled and said, "I'll be the talk of the town tomorrow."

Paul and Jeff stayed the night in one of Beth's other rooms and were planning to leave the next morning. "No, stay and join Joseph and me for lunch. I'd like for you all to meet," I pleaded.

Jeff tried to hide his smirk but was unsuccessful. Paul looked from Jeff to me and agreed. "I'd like to meet the illustrious Joseph," he said, trying to be nonchalant.

"Well, it's settled then. You two will join us for lunch before you go home." Paul and Jeff exchanged a brief but meaningful look. I got suspicious and asked, "You aren't planning on interrogating him, are you?"

Paul walked away, saying, "I make no promises. After the last idiot you dated, I've decided to become the Southern man my mama created me to be."

"You mean woman," I shouted, as he was already halfway down the hallway before he finished talking.

I looked at Jeff and asked, "What do you two have planned? Joseph is a sensitive man, and I don't want you two chasing him off."

Beth walked into the kitchen just as I was finishing that statement and said, "Joseph knows family have questions, hell, we interrogated the shit out of you." I couldn't argue with her, but I decided to text Joseph beforehand and warn him to be prepared.

Joseph showed up right at noon. He was dressed to meet family. Instead of the old carpenter pants and t-shirt he usually wore, he had on slacks and a button-down shirt. I cocked my eyebrow at him when he walked in and leaned over to whisper, "Why don't you ever dress up for me like this?"

"Because," he whispered back, "when I'm with you, I figure I'm going to just get naked anyway, so no use dressing up."

I chuckled. "Sorta full of yourself, aren't you?"

He shook his head and said, "No, just hopeful."

I led him into the living room where Beth, Paul and Jeff were sitting.

"Jeff, Paul, this is Joseph. Joseph, this is Paul, my brother, and his husband, Jeff."

"Nice to meet you both," Joseph said with a sincere smile. I owed it to my brother, he didn't begin the interrogation right away but as soon as we'd sat down at the restaurant, the questions began.

"What do you do for a living?"

"Did you grow up here?"

"Have you ever lived anywhere else?"

"How many men have you dated?"

I intervened at that one and told Joseph he didn't have to answer, which my brother quickly refuted and said that as the oldest sibling and since Dad was no longer around, it was his duty to ask.

Joseph just smiled and answered, "Several, but not a lot."

I nodded my approval. "Good answer."

It didn't take Paul long to wind down, however, and Joseph's good nature won him over. Joseph never got upset, angry, or even perturbed by my brother's nosey questions, but rather sat back and answered them as honestly as possible. I was very proud of him and very ready for my brother to go home. At one point, during the interrogation, I even said as much. Jeff choked with the comment and almost spit water through his nose.

The rest of lunch went great. Paul and Jeff seemed to like Joseph, and he seemed to like them. They didn't have a lot in common, Paul and Jeff being artists and Joseph being an outdoorsman and ranger. Still, they had me in common, and inevitably, that's what the conversation turned to. Much to my chagrin, my overprotective brother began asking Joseph about the incident where I'd been hit. I quickly chimed in that Joseph hadn't been with me, trying to avoid any discussion about us having fought.

Then, to my utter dismay, he actually said he was partially to blame for the accident and told my brother that we had been in an argument before I went for a run.

"Joseph, dammit, you aren't to blame. We had a tiff because of a stupid misunderstanding, that's all," I said, turning to Paul and Jeff. "I was trying to give Joseph space that he didn't want, and he thought I was avoiding him. So, simple mistake, and we've cleared it up. I'm the only person to blame for going out running late at night without some kind of reflector on and not paying better attention to what was going on around me. That is it, end of story."

My brother looked at me, then at Joseph. "Listen, everyone argues, but something fishy is going on. Joseph, did you hear that we'd been broken into?" Joseph nodded. "Did you know the only thing the perp did was take a knife to Daniel's clothing, cutting out the crotch of his underwear?"

Joseph looked over at me and shook his head.

"Did you know someone tried to follow Daniel the next day, and he had to call the cops to pull the jackass over?"

Again, Joseph looked at me and shook his head.

"So, you can see why we are more than a little concerned about this hit-and-run, as it were. If someone is targeting Daniel, we want to make sure he's safe."

All I could do was put my head in my hands and wait for the embarrassment to pass. Through my hands, I said, "First of all, they aren't related, and second, I'm a grown-ass man. Joseph isn't gonna babysit me, and I don't need to be babysat! Paul, why are you blowing this up out of proportion?"

"I'm not blowing anything out of proportion," Paul said, his face turning red.

I could tell the Southern bomb, that was my brother, was about to explode when Jeff put his hand over Paul's and said to me, "Daniel, we know you are grown. Of course, we know that. It isn't like we want to control you or tell you what to do, but we love you. You've been through so much these past few months. Your ex cheated on you with a psychopath, you fell off a mountain, then the break-in and now the hit-and-run. You're our family and both of us, especially your brother, are worried sick about you. You have to let us worry over you a bit. That's what it means to be family."

Damn, I hated when Jeff used his reasonable sensibilities against me. "I know you both love me, and I promise, cross my heart and hope *not* to die, that I won't put myself in another dangerous situation."

"If he'll let me, I'll make sure of it," Joseph added. "I've asked Daniel to come stay with me. I live in a small cabin out in a very remote area, so he'll be secluded and protected. No one even knows the cabin is there. Even the Postal Service delivers mail to the ranger station. The cabin doesn't even have an official mailing address."

I couldn't help but chuckle at my brother's expression. I could only imagine what he thought about staying in a secluded cabin in the backwoods somewhere, since we both grew up in the backwoods of rural Tennessee.

"I haven't agreed to stay with Joseph yet," I said, giving Joseph a meaningful look. "But if I do, the cabin is really nice. It's a little bungalow and it's been kept up well. It isn't a scary Tennessee cabin." I could see I'd hit the mark for my brother, and he smiled.

Then he turned to Joseph. "I don't know if secluded is safer or not. If someone is trying to hurt Daniel, I doubt a dirt road would stop them. In fact, it might make them more dangerous. Regardless, if you promise me you will try to see that Daniel isn't alone or in a compromised position, at least until all the court stuff is done, I'd appreciate it." Then he reached over and took Jeff's hand and corrected himself, "We'd appreciate it."

I was touched by the fact that my tough brother and brother-in-law were concerned enough to ask that of someone they just met. I liked the idea that they trusted Joseph enough to ask him, but I didn't like the idea of people watching over me, and I said just that.

"I'm not going to tolerate anyone watching over my shoulder." Then I pointed at Joseph and said, "I want none of that getting your family to surreptitiously watch me like I'm under police protection or something."

Joseph looked down, and I knew that was exactly what he'd intended to ask them to do. "If someone is trying to hurt me, which is highly unlikely," I added, "then I'll be more than safe under Beth's watch and while I'm working with Kaden."

I looked over at my brother and said, "Not to mention, I can take care of myself. I'm from the rural South and have been shooting guns since I was knee-high!"

My brother huffed. "How many guns do you have access to?"

"Well, none," I admitted. "But if one was handy and I was being attacked, I'd know how to use it."

We all sat staring at each other for a moment, then the humor of the last statement made all four of us laugh.

Finally, after the laughter died down, Paul reached over and patted my head, like he used to do when I was younger.

"I don't care how you stay safe, little brother. I just want to make sure that you do."

I put my hand up like we did during Boy Scouts and said, "On my honor, I will not put myself in any more danger and that I will be safe." Paul chuckled again, and just like that we were good.

Paul and Jeff left for Edmonds instead of going back to Beth's, and Joseph drove me back to the bed and breakfast. When we got to the house, both Beth and Kaden were sitting at the kitchen island.

"Dad, Aunt B," Joseph began. "Paul and Jeff are concerned these incidents between the break-in and the hit-and-run are linked. I would like your opinion." I glared at Joseph, but he ignored me. "I think my place is safer than here, there's only one way in, and you'd have to know the area really well to even know the cabin is back there. There are no trails leading to the cabin, and from the main road, it's at least a five-mile hike through the woods to get to it. Until we know that he's safe, do you agree that my place would be the safest?"

I continued to glare at Joseph, and I saw out of the corner of my eye that both Beth and Kaden were amused. Finally, Kaden cleared his throat. "If someone were trying to hurt me or someone I cared about, I think the cabin would be the safest place possible, but son, that kind of seclusion isn't for everyone."

Beth nodded in agreement. "Joseph, Daniel might prefer more modern accommodations, and I think it is safe enough here. We have a security system that I could start using if that would make you feel more comfortable."

Joseph nodded.

"It does make me more comfortable, Aunt B. Dad, it would also make me more comfortable if you didn't leave Daniel alone at the shop."

I never stopped glaring at Joseph, and I was becoming angry enough that I was sure my Southern roots were going to cause me to explode. For some reason, my usual angry explosion never happened. Instead, I sat down on the stool, catty-corner to the three of them, crossed my arms, and said, "When the three of you decide how I'm to live my life for the next few weeks, do please be kind enough to let me know."

Beth looked down, stifling a snicker, and Kaden looked over at her.

"Why don't we give these two some space before Daniel explodes all over our boy and we get struck by shrapnel," he said.

"What a lovely idea," Beth said, and the two of them left the kitchen.

I continued staring at Joseph, who didn't seem to be the least bit concerned. "So, what happened to you not bringing the rest of the family into the conversation?" I asked.

"That was your idea," Joseph said. "I never agreed to it."

"Joseph, I may let my brother get away with being bossy, telling me what to do, but I'm damn well not gonna let my lover get away with that kind of stuff. I won't be told to stay with you, or here, or anything else. I admit, I've gotten myself into a kind of predicament with the idiots I hung out with in Seattle, but at the end of the day, the worst thing I did was punch a son of a bitch in the face. I haven't done anything to anyone to want to hurt me. It's absolutely ridiculous that last night's hit-and-run was anything other than a drunk driver being stupid."

Joseph came toward me, and I could see the concern on his face. I put my hand up to force him to stop and added, "I appreciate that you're concerned, and if anything else strange happens, I will be sure to add more security measures. But for now, all we have are some random and extreme circumstances and nothing to prove that there's anything to be concerned about. Besides that, the likelihood that Nathan or Tony know where I am, or even care where I am, is very slim."

Joseph finished crossing the floor between us and put his arms around my sullen form, then kissed me on the forehead right on the sore spot.

"I won't pretend that I don't agree with your brother, and I won't lie and tell you I don't feel very protective of you right now. But I will promise to back off a little bit, unless something else happens," he said.

"Now, the truth is I want you in my bed at night. I only have you here for a couple more weeks, and if you end up going back to Seattle, I want to take advantage of every night you are here. If that means I can keep you safe and have access to you so we can hopefully have a lot more sex, then what's the downside?" he asked. "So, what do you say?"

"I say that for the nights you are going to be home, sure, I'll agree to stay with you. But the nights you have to work, I'll stay here at Beth's. That way, if you need some"–I almost said *space* but quickly changed the words to avoid that subject again –"times to yourself, you don't always have to worry about entertaining me. Besides, if I didn't have some time with Beth, I'd miss her."

In the next room, Beth hollered out, "That's right, we need girlfriend time."

Joseph and I laughed, realizing our entire conversation had been overheard. "I'll drive my car to your house, so you don't have to drive me back and forth to Kaden's every day. She's a piece of shit, but at least she'll make that drive with little problem."

Joseph pulled me into his arms and kissed me hard. "I'm so happy," he said and was so enthusiastic I couldn't help but laugh.

"I'm looking forward to having more naked time with you too," I whispered so eavesdroppers couldn't hear.

I packed my belongings in case Beth could rent the room out while I was at Joseph's, and put the luggage in the back of my car. I followed Joseph, and we stopped off at an ice cream place and sat down by the old shops facing the Salish Sea and ate as we chatted.

Joseph wrapped his arms around me, and I snuggled in as if I were on autopilot. Joseph's PDA felt so right, so appropriate, that I didn't even seem to notice. Under normal circumstances, I would have felt like a freak in the open with my lover's arms around me.

Like most small towns, Port Angeles turned into a ghost town late in the afternoon and early evening on a Sunday. There were a few stragglers wandering around when we'd finally finished our ice creams and got up to leave. I'd just got back in the car to follow Joseph when I noticed a white sedan parked behind me. I thought I recognized it as the same one that followed me in Edmonds, so I called Joseph and told him my suspicion. He directed me to drive up the block and gave me directions to the County Sheriff's Office.

"I want you to drive slowly to the Sheriff's Office. On the way, call nine-one-one and tell them what you suspect. Meanwhile, I'll wait for you to pass and see if the guy follows you. If he does, I'll snap a picture of his license plate," he said.

I did as he instructed, and sure enough, the car pulled out right after I did and started following me. I called nine-one-one and told the dispatcher what was happening and that my friend was following behind the stranger in order to get a picture of the license plate.

The dispatcher told me to continue as we'd planned, then pull into the Sheriff's Office to see what happened. I did as she instructed, and as soon as I pulled into the parking lot of the station, the car floored the gas and sped past. Joseph pulled in behind me, parking his car next to mine. When he got out, he showed me the picture and asked, "Does this look like the car that hit you?"

I shook my head and repeated what I'd already told everyone, "I don't remember much about the vehicle that hit me, only that it was a sedan. We went into the Sheriff's Office, and a deputy came out to speak with us. Joseph ended up sending the picture to the deputy's mobile, and he told us he'd let us know what came back from the plates.

No surprise, the deputy knew Joseph and offered to follow us out to Joseph's driveway just to ensure no one followed. I tried to wave him off, saying it was probably nothing. Joseph overrode me again and told the guy that would probably be a good idea. I just shook my head and thought how embarrassing it was.

The deputy followed us all the way out to Joseph's, and as far as I could tell, no one else followed us. When we pulled down the mostly dirt road that was Joseph's driveway, the deputy got out and came inside the cabin with us.

"They ran the plates at the station, and we got the name. Does a James McAllister ring a bell?" he asked me.

I looked at the deputy in shock. "Yeah, that's my ex-boss. He owned the bar I worked at until he fired me."

The deputy nodded. "I'm going to give the police department in Edmonds a call and see what they know about this guy, and check to see if he's the same one that runs the bar you work at. Until then, you'll need to be careful. I'm not sure why this guy is following you or even if it is him, but if it is, he could have some weird thing going on. I'd prefer you to be safe than sorry."

I just shook my head. "Why would Mr. McAllister give a damn about me being in Port Angeles?"

Then it struck me. He'd had a crush on Nathan. Before the deputy turned to leave, I said, "Mr. McAllister had a crush on a guy I decked in the nose when I caught him kissing my boyfriend. I wouldn't be at all surprised if Nathan hasn't put him up to all this."

"We'll check into that too," he said. "For now, you are about as safe out here as you can be. I doubt anyone could find this place even if they were looking and had a map."

Joseph just looked at the deputy with a *fuck you* look on his face. "Yeah, we've heard that all before, Doug. Get some original stuff, will ya?"

Doug, the deputy sheriff, just chuckled. "You all be safe and let us know if you need anything."

"Thanks, deputy," I said. As he walked back to his car, I asked Joseph how he knew Doug.

Joseph laughed. "I'm related to him somehow, but mostly, we spent our summers together. He likes to make fun of where I live."

Then Joseph winked at me. "That is until he wants to bring a hot date to my hot tub in the woods."

I looked at Joseph like he'd just swallowed a whole watermelon. "You let other people have sex in our hot tub?"

"I've let a few," he admitted. "But only a select few, and until you, I'd never used it myself. Besides, Doug and a few other friends already knew about the pool. We used to slip down here when old Mr. Bowechop lived here. He was our third or fourth cousin... something like two times removed, and said he didn't mind if we parked in his driveway and hiked up to the pool. By then he was so old, I doubted he ever went up there anyway."

"I still don't like the idea of our place being sullied by straight teenagers," I replied.

Joseph chuckled and grabbed me in a hug. "I promise I'll scare off all horny teenagers from now on."

"And what about horny deputy sheriffs?" I asked.

"Considering Mary, his wife, is pregnant with their third child, I don't think it'll be much of a concern."

I grinned. "Good," I said. "That is *our* horny sex spot."

"How about we go up there now?" Joseph said, wagging his eyebrows.

"Help me take my stuff in, and I'll race you." Then I absent-mindedly rubbed my sore head and said, "By race, I meant walk slowly so I don't make my headache come back."

Joseph looked at my head. "Yeah, maybe hot springs tonight isn't the best idea. Let's try it tomorrow night after my dad works the legs off you."

"Yeah," I said. "Don't remind me. This bump on my head put some real skids on all the sex I intended to have with you this weekend."

"We can make up for that right now," Joseph said.

"Yes, please," I said, and we dropped my stuff inside the door and made for the bedroom.

That night, our lovemaking was gentle and sweet. I could tell Joseph was still taking care of me, but I could also tell he needed to take the lead, so I let him. When he took me, unlike our first time, he rode me slowly. I could feel the love coming out of him as he moved inside me.

After sex, we both showered and cuddled in front of the old stone fireplace in his living room, my head in his lap. I dozed on and off as the fire crackled.

When he woke me by shifting his body to get more comfortable, I grinned up at him then turned over, taking his cock out of his sweats and giving him a blowjob. I'd always wanted to do that, just lazily take a guy I cared about in my mouth, just to hear him moan.

I pushed his cock deep into my throat, enjoying the way it felt as it hit against the back. I'd long ago lost my gag reflex, and a cock in my throat had become something I enjoyed. Of course, none as much as I liked Joseph's big thick cock.

I loved how he climaxed with me giving him a blowjob. His moans of pleasure plunging my heart deeper and deeper into the point of no return. When I swallowed, Joseph arched back and softly called my name. When he came in my mouth tonight, he pushed me back onto the sofa, laid on top of me, and kissed me long and hard. I ended up coming as he fucked his still hard cock into me as we lay together.

I lifted off him, and he leaned over, kissing me. "You touch my heart, Daniel."

I smiled. "You touch mine too."

The three big words weren't said, it was still too early, but the feeling was clearly the same for both of us.

That night, I slept deep and contented.

Twelve

ON FRIDAY AFTERNOON, DOUG, the deputy who escorted Joseph and me out to his place, showed up at Kaden's workshop right before the two of us knocked off for the day. He said he'd heard back from the Edmonds Police. My former boss was indeed the same guy they'd pulled over in Edmonds when I was headed here.

They were also concerned because there was still an active investigation going on with Mr. McAllister, who remained a person of interest in relation to the crap that went down in Seattle last year when I worked at his bar.

Somehow, he'd figured out I was in Port Angeles, and they were looking for him to question where he was the night of the hit-and-run. I asked about Nathan, and the deputy said that both he and Mr. McAllister were missing.

"Damn," I said. "So, you think the two of them are in this together?"

Doug just shrugged and said, "There isn't any way to know for sure, but there's an APB out for both of them to be brought in for questioning."

I asked if my ex-boyfriend Tony had been contacted about Nathan, and again the deputy shrugged. "I don't know who all they've spoken to, but they are taking this pretty seriously so, I imagine they've turned over every rock."

I reminded the deputy that we had court one week from Monday. I doubted Nathan would skip that since he was fairly certain he was going to be able to put me in jail for a little while. The deputy smiled and said, "Under the circumstances, I think your friend is the one who should be concerned about jail time."

"He's no friend of mine," I assured him, but agreed about the circumstances.

Doug reminded me to remain vigilant.

"If you see anyone following you, be careful," he said. "Once you get on the backroads to Joseph's place, there aren't many places to go for help." I nodded, and he left.

Kaden came over and sat on the stool across from the desk I was sitting at.

"We need to let Joseph know things have gotten a bit hotter around this," he said.

"I'll let him know tonight. Mr. McCoy," I said, "I may need to lay low until after court."

I was beginning to feel a little frightened by all the circumstances. It still seemed strange that Nathan or my former boss were trying to hurt me. I mean, the entire situation was minor in the scheme of things, so I couldn't wrap my brain around why they were escalating it to this level. Maybe things would become clear after court.

Kaden looked at me with his concerned parent look and agreed. "We'll have Joseph bring you here when he can, or I'll pick you up from his place. I agree, we better not have you on the road alone until we know more about those two."

Kaden ended up following me home that night, which was frustrating since I knew he wanted to go see Sam. When I got to Joseph's, he was standing at the door of the cabin. Seeing him never failed to bring a feeling of safety and security. My heart leaped every single time I was reunited with him. Trying not to make an ass of myself in front of Kaden, I walked up to Joseph and kissed him before going inside. Kaden stopped to talk to Joseph. I assumed it was to inform him that the deputy had stopped by. I put my stuff in the living room and came out to join them. Kaden was telling Joseph that one of them should be with me at all times until things settled down, and Joseph was nodding.

"I'm really sorry about this, guys," I said, shaking my head. "I feel like a helpless damsel in distress over all this. I can't say I'm not nervous, though. Things seem to be getting out of hand."

Joseph put his arm around me and pulled me close. "You don't need to feel bad. When they catch these guys, you'll feel safer again, and we'll put an end to this once and for all."

The worry and frustration of getting them involved weighed heavily on me. I looked up at Joseph. His strong arm around me and his expression of concern seemed to take some of the stress out of the situation. As long as I was with Joseph, I knew I'd be okay.

Kaden left, but not without reminding us that it was better to stay safe than be sorry. We went into the cabin, and Joseph sat down, opening his schedule on his phone. He wrote down the days he wouldn't be available to get me to work and suggested I stay with Beth those nights.

"I don't want you to," he said. "But like Dad said, I'd rather be safe than sorry."

I felt so helpless. All I could do was sit there like a dumb-ass and let my life be dictated by people I'd only recently met. I hated being an inconvenience, but that's all I'd been since my arrival. How could they still want me around?

Joseph noticed I was distracted. He put his phone down and came over to sit on the chair next to me.

"I know this is hard," he said. "But it'll be over soon, you'll see."

I just sat there. I didn't know what to say. Finally, without looking at Joseph, I said what was on my mind.

"Joseph, since we met, I've been nothing but one massive problem after another. First, I fell off the mountain and broke my arm, then I was stuck at your aunt's house for weeks while I healed, then this crap with Nathan and Mr. McAllister. It doesn't seem that I can catch a break, and I'm pulling all of you into my drama."

Joseph shook his head as he pulled my face around to look at him.

"We care about you, Daniel," he said. "You are one of us. This is how it works sometimes. The universe puts us into each other's paths when we need each other the most. I know it hurts your pride to depend on us, but if we didn't care about you, we wouldn't have volunteered to take this on."

"How can you all care so much when we barely know each other?" I asked, standing up and pacing around the room. "I was a stranger to all of you just a few weeks back. Now you're taking on things like making sure I don't drive alone to a job your dad gave me out of pity. I just don't understand what's in this for all of you."

Joseph stood up and came over, holding my arms while he spoke. "Daniel, that's horseshit, and you know it. Think about it for a minute. Do you think my Aunt B is the kind of woman who'd preen over just anyone?"

I thought about it for a minute and couldn't help but smile. Beth was no pushover.

I shook my head. "No, she probably wouldn't."

"So, you know the only reason she's so open to you coming into her home is because she cares about you," he said, and I nodded. "Now think about my dad. Do you really think that man would let you come into his place of business, which he guards like the three-headed dog guards the gates of Hades, if you weren't pulling your weight there?"

"No," I said chuckling. Kaden was almost as intense about his workshop as Beth was over her home.

"Now, look at me, Daniel." I looked at him. "If I didn't really care about you, if I didn't want you here, in my life, do you think

I would have brought you here, would have asked you to stay?" he asked.

That one was harder. Did Joseph really care about me, or was it a pity situation?

"Joseph, I know how *I* feel about *you*, but I admit, I don't know... not really, about us... I know it isn't fair to compare you to my past, but I've trusted others who have pretended to care but ended up being hateful, even evil. Look at the situation I'm in right now. Nathan was supposed to be my closest friend, and now, every ounce of evidence points to him wanting to cause me harm, and for what? My punching him for kissing my boyfriend?"

Joseph pulled back and looked at me hard. "I can't force you to understand my feelings for you, and I can't force you to trust me, Daniel. I can only be myself and hope that eventually, you'll see me for who and what I am."

I could tell he was hurt as he let me go and walked outside. I wished I could go to him, tell him I loved him, but the situation with Nathan was raw, and I was hurting too much myself. I went to his bedroom and laid down, willing the emotional pain to stop and to give myself some time to think about how to comfort Joseph without lying about my feelings or fears.

I ended up falling asleep. I woke up to the smell of bacon, and when I walked out of the bedroom, I found Joseph at the stove, cooking. When he saw me, he said, "I figured I'd fix us breakfast for dinner tonight."

"My mom used to do that," I said and smiled at him.

"Joseph," I began. "I apologize for before, but..." Joseph turned from the stove and interrupted me.

"No, you don't need to apologize. Of course, you're struggling with trust issues right now. I can imagine what it must be like dealing with the fallout from your friend turned enemy. I'm in this for the long-term, Daniel. We're friends first, and that means a lot to me. Being your lover just makes that more difficult to accept, and I know that, so I want you to know you have all the time you need." Joseph turned the stove off, came over to where I stood and leaned over to kiss me. "Okay?" he asked.

I nodded. "Okay."

The rest of the night was much nicer. We went back up to the hot springs and soaked a while, then we came back to the cabin and made love twice.

We spent the weekend putzing around the cabin. We went for a few hikes through the woods, and Joseph showed me some of his favorite spots in the area. We even went fishing off his little harbor, and I was surprised that we brought in a nice-size coho salmon.

"Can we keep that to eat?" I asked Joseph.

"I'll have to register it with the state, but yeah, we can eat it." He smiled.

If you've never eaten fresh wild salmon, you have no idea what you're missing. Joseph took the fish and cleaned it, then went through a long process to prepare it. I eventually sat down on a reclining chair he had outside and watched him. He was steeped in knowledge about all the animals, fish, and plants in the area, and I loved listening to him slip into ranger mode as he described what we'd seen, or in this case, caught.

He was talking about how there was a growing fear that the orca, which usually survived on salmon and other fish, would eventually starve if conservation efforts weren't strictly in place. As he was talking, I dozed off.

In my dream, I was somewhere in the national park, the snowy owl perched on a nearby branch. I could tell it was concerned. I began to walk down one of the trails when I heard screaming. I could tell it was a man, but I couldn't tell where it was coming from. I began looking for the person, moving in the direction I'd heard the sound but never finding where the person was.

Exhausted, I sat down on a boulder and put my head in my hands and started to cry. When I looked up, Mr. McAllister was standing in front of me, covered in blood. He had an evil smile on his face and was carrying a large knife like a machete. When he saw me looking at him, he smiled even wider and said, "You're next."

When he lunged at me, I woke up. I was panting, and I could feel the sweat sticking to me. Joseph heard me and came over.

"What's wrong?" he asked.

I looked at Joseph in dread and said, "I think Mr. McAllister killed Nathan. I think I heard him kill Nathan!"

I figured Joseph would think I'm nuts. I didn't tell people about my dreams. Most of the time, there wasn't much to tell, but all my family had some sort of the sight. We usually laughed about how useless it was because it never really told us useful stuff like what lottery numbers would win or who would win the World Series.

Joseph looked at me concerned. He questioned me about the specifics of my dream, and I told him every part that I could remember.

"You say you think it happened in the park?" he asked.

"Yeah," I answered. After having fully woken up, I reached over to Joseph and put my hand on his arm. "It was just a dream, Joseph," I said. "I had a bad dream, that's all. All this crazy stuff about Nathan and Mr. McAllister just has me messed up in the head. Why would Mr. McAllister want to kill Nathan?"

Joseph came over and stood next to me. "Don't be so quick to toss away a warning. I've found when there are messages we're supposed to hear, the spirits tend to send them to us through our dreams. The fact that your spirit animal, the owl you told me about, was present confirms that for me."

I hadn't called the owl my animal spirit or guide or anything. I wasn't full-blooded Native American, and I knew so many people wanted to run roughshod over their cultures that I never claimed such things. My grandma had called the owl my spirit guide though, so I wasn't in a place to argue with Joseph about it.

"I'll let the guys know down at the ranger station that we need to comb the trails to see if there's any sign of your former boss or friend. I won't tell them about the dream, just that we have two missing people, one of whom was seen in town recently."

Then we both walked inside. When he got his phone, he said, "I probably should have already done that." He took his phone outside the cabin, and I could hear him as he talked to the ranger about his concern. When he came back in, he told me they were going to send out some scouts and that they'd ask the helicopter pilots, who make the rounds with tourists, to pay close attention to the trails for any possible hikers we weren't aware of.

Joseph finished prepping the salmon in the kitchen and came over to the sofa, I was now lying on and lifting my head to slide in under me. I snuggled closer to him.

"It was pretty scary to see Mr. McAllister covered in blood," I said. "Do you think it is possible that he really has killed Nathan?"

Joseph shook his head while running his fingers through my hair. "I don't know. If your dream was a warning, it could've just been telling you he's capable of murder, or it could be warning you that there was a murder. I've come to see that when a spirit sends a warning, it isn't always exactly what happened or is about to happen."

I nodded, and as I remembered the dream, I was relieved to have Joseph close to me.

When the buzzer went off on the old stove, we got up and went to the dinner table. Joseph pulled the salmon out, and while it rested, he tossed some asparagus into a hot frying pan.

The salmon was possibly one of the most fantastic-tasting foods I've ever put in my mouth.

"How did you learn to cook this way?" I asked.

Joseph's smile was sad. "My mother was known to be the best cook around. She loved wild-caught salmon and had several ways of fixing it. This was my favorite, so I got her to teach me. Every time I catch salmon, I think of her," he said.

After eating, I prompted Joseph to tell me more about his mom. I could tell how much he loved her as he told one fun story about her after another.

—————

Monday morning came too soon. Joseph was scheduled to work during the day and needed to accompany a group of scientists who had come in from Boston to see some of the wildlife in the national park. He knew he wouldn't be available much while they were there, so he asked me to leave my car. He'd drive me into town, and then Kaden would be in charge of getting me back and forth to Beth's place.

I won't pretend I didn't hate that I was being toted around like a child again, but I tried not to complain. I knew we only had one week before the court date and then, if I was lucky, we'd get everything squared away.

Of course, I couldn't have been more wrong. I stayed at Beth's until Thursday morning, helping Kaden during the day and then hanging out with Beth in the evenings. The two of them watched me like a hawk. Despite the fact I'd come to love the two of them, and they felt more like family than friends, I was ready to do myself in and save Nathan or Mr. McAllister the trouble.

On Wednesday I got a call from Joseph saying they'd found Mr. McAllister's car hidden at one of the trailheads. It had been covered in branches and debris, so people who'd driven by had missed seeing it. The Sheriff's Office had towed it into town and were doing a sweep to see what they could find.

"Well," I said to Joseph, "that means they are probably up on the mountain somewhere." Despite the warmth of the shop, I felt myself shiver. Their finding the car seemed to confirm my premonition was not just a dream, after all.

They found Nathan's body the following day. Just as in my dream, he'd been killed with a knife of some kind. Finding Nathan put the entire county and National Park Service law enforcement rangers on high alert. Helicopters were flying over the mountain in the manhunt. I was worried about Beth being alone with me. I called Joseph and told him I wasn't comfortable staying at her place, and putting her at risk. He said the Boston scientists left today because of the safety concern and that he'd be over to pick me up after he'd finished some of his duties at the park.

I called Beth and told her what our plans were and asked that she make sure to keep her house locked and alarmed until the guy was caught.

"If he is after me," I told her, "he might use you as a way to get to me. Please don't take chances, Mrs. Beth."

She agreed she would take precautions, but she was more concerned about me at the moment.

"I'll be fine at Joseph's," I told her. "We're more secluded there, and it's unlikely the guy will be able to find me."

I didn't go back to Kaden's for the rest of the week but stayed with Joseph. He kept tabs on the search and investigation, but nothing had turned up. By the time Sunday night arrived, I was ready to get back to Seattle. The police agreed to meet me at the station Monday morning, and an officer would escort me into court. We already knew that Nathan was dead, but if Mr. McAllister knew we had court, he might be willing to come out of hiding or follow me there.

I convinced Joseph that I was fine to go on my own, which he was not at all keen on.

"Joseph, what are you going to do that I can't do on the way down there?" I asked. "You can come with me to fill my tank up, then I'll be alone in the car until I get to Seattle. If I have any trouble, I'll alert the authorities. Everyone is on the lookout for the guy, so he's more likely than not hiding somewhere up in the mountains. Besides, as far as we know, he doesn't have a car, and if he does find one, he won't know where I'm coming from. I really think we're fine with me going down alone."

Joseph was upset, but he'd been called in to the ranger station to help man a few of the different trails. Until the manhunt was over, the rangers were asked to patrol in twos. With the cuts to the Park Service, they really didn't have enough rangers for him not to be there, or at least somewhere in the park, so he'd begrudgingly agreed.

The drive down to Seattle was uneventful, as I'd guessed it would be. I phoned the Officer Sparks who'd gotten himself assigned to me as I was getting ready to turn into the station, and he met me outside the building. My court case was scheduled for eleven in the morning, and it was already ten-fifteen, so I asked him if he could follow me to the courthouse.

There were no suspicious cars following me, and when I got to the courthouse, Todd, Paul and Jeff were waiting for me at the door to the courtroom. Paul grabbed me into a hug, which still felt strange to me, but I knew he was concerned about the whole Nathan thing.

Officer Sparks escorted us all into the courtroom, and when the judge came in, Todd told him what had happened to Nathan. The judge was alarmed by the news. "You say he was killed up where you were staying?"

"I was staying outside the national park, and he was killed somewhere in the park. The County Sheriff's Office has a suspect, but they're still doing a manhunt to find him."

The judge nodded. "Son, I'm not sure you should've come in today. It might have been better for you to have your attorney call in and request a dismissal, considering the circumstances."

"Yes, Your Honor," I said. "But we were hoping by coming here today, it might flush out the suspect."

The judge dismissed the case and wished me luck.

There was no sign of Mr. McAllister, so I decided to spend the night with my brother and Jeff instead of trying to go all the way back to Port Angeles. Even though the court outcome was predictable, I was exhausted from all the drama around it. I felt horrible about Nathan, and when I closed my eyes, all I could see was Mr. McAllister covered in blood... Nathan's blood.

Yeah, he'd been a horrible friend, but he didn't deserve to die like that. No one deserved to die like that.

Jeff and Paul followed me back to the house and forced me to park my junker in the garage. "That's safer," they said. We ate dinner with little discussion, all of us thinking about the events of the past few days.

Paul asked questions about the folks in Port Angeles while we poked at the pizza we'd ordered. Finally, I told the guys that I just wanted to turn in. So, I went to bed early and texted Joseph.

Hey honey, the day went well. I'm getting ready for bed. I can't wait to see you tomorrow.

Joseph texted back immediately.

Sleep well.

O

n Friday afternoon, Doug, the deputy who escorted Joseph and me out to his place, showed up at Kaden's workshop right before the two of us knocked off for the day. He said he'd heard back from the Edmonds Police. My former boss was indeed the same guy they'd pulled over in Edmonds when I was headed here.

They were also concerned because there was still an active investigation going on with Mr. McAllister, who remained a person of interest in relation to the crap that went down in Seattle last year when I worked at his bar.

Somehow, he'd figured out I was in Port Angeles, and they were looking for him to question where he was the night of the hit-and-run. I asked about Nathan, and the deputy said that both he and Mr. McAllister were missing.

"Damn," I said. "So, you think the two of them are in this together?"

Doug just shrugged and said, "There isn't any way to know for sure, but there's an APB out for both of them to be brought in for questioning."

I asked if my ex-boyfriend Tony had been contacted about Nathan, and again the deputy shrugged. "I don't know who all they've spoken to, but they are taking this pretty seriously so, I imagine they've turned over every rock."

I reminded the deputy that we had court one week from Monday. I doubted Nathan would skip that since he was fairly certain he was going to be able to put me in jail for a little while. The deputy smiled and said, "Under the circumstances, I think your friend is the one who should be concerned about jail time."

"He's no friend of mine," I assured him, but agreed about the circumstances.

Doug reminded me to remain vigilant.

"If you see anyone following you, be careful," he said. "Once you get on the backroads to Joseph's place, there aren't many places to go for help." I nodded, and he left.

Kaden came over and sat on the stool across from the desk I was sitting at.

"We need to let Joseph know things have gotten a bit hotter around this," he said.

"I'll let him know tonight. Mr. McCoy," I said, "I may need to lay low until after court."

I was beginning to feel a little frightened by all the circumstances. It still seemed strange that Nathan or my former boss were trying to hurt me. I mean, the entire situation was minor in the scheme of things, so I couldn't wrap my brain around why they were escalating it to this level. Maybe things would become clear after court.

Kaden looked at me with his concerned parent look and agreed. "We'll have Joseph bring you here when he can, or I'll pick you up from his place. I agree, we better not have you on the road alone until we know more about those two."

Kaden ended up following me home that night, which was frustrating since I knew he wanted to go see Sam. When I got to Joseph's, he was standing at the door of the cabin. Seeing him never failed to bring a feeling of safety and security. My heart leaped every single time I was reunited with him. Trying not to make an ass of myself in front of Kaden, I walked up to Joseph and kissed him before going inside. Kaden stopped to talk to Joseph. I assumed it was to inform him that the deputy had stopped by. I put my stuff in the living room and came out to join them. Kaden was telling Joseph that one of them should be with me at all times until things settled down, and Joseph was nodding.

"I'm really sorry about this, guys," I said, shaking my head. "I feel like a helpless damsel in distress over all this. I can't say I'm not nervous, though. Things seem to be getting out of hand."

Joseph put his arm around me and pulled me close. "You don't need to feel bad. When they catch these guys, you'll feel safer again, and we'll put an end to this once and for all."

The worry and frustration of getting them involved weighed heavily on me. I looked up at Joseph. His strong arm around me and his expression of concern seemed to take some of the stress out of the situation. As long as I was with Joseph, I knew I'd be okay.

Kaden left, but not without reminding us that it was better to stay safe than be sorry. We went into the cabin, and Joseph sat down, opening his schedule on his phone. He wrote down the days he wouldn't be available to get me to work and suggested I stay with Beth those nights.

"I don't want you to," he said. "But like Dad said, I'd rather be safe than sorry."

I felt so helpless. All I could do was sit there like a dumb-ass and let my life be dictated by people I'd only recently met. I hated being an inconvenience, but that's all I'd been since my arrival. How could they still want me around?

Joseph noticed I was distracted. He put his phone down and came over to sit on the chair next to me.

"I know this is hard," he said. "But it'll be over soon, you'll see."

I just sat there. I didn't know what to say. Finally, without looking at Joseph, I said what was on my mind.

"Joseph, since we met, I've been nothing but one massive problem after another. First, I fell off the mountain and broke my arm, then I was stuck at your aunt's house for weeks while I healed, then this crap with Nathan and Mr. McAllister. It doesn't seem that I can catch a break, and I'm pulling all of you into my drama."

Joseph shook his head as he pulled my face around to look at him.

"We care about you, Daniel," he said. "You are one of us. This is how it works sometimes. The universe puts us into each other's paths when we need each other the most. I know it hurts your pride to depend on us, but if we didn't care about you, we wouldn't have volunteered to take this on."

"How can you all care so much when we barely know each other?" I asked, standing up and pacing around the room. "I was a stranger to all of you just a few weeks back. Now you're taking on things like making sure I don't drive alone to a job your dad gave me out of pity. I just don't understand what's in this for all of you."

Joseph stood up and came over, holding my arms while he spoke. "Daniel, that's horseshit, and you know it. Think about it for a minute. Do you think my Aunt B is the kind of woman who'd preen over just anyone?"

I thought about it for a minute and couldn't help but smile. Beth was no pushover.

I shook my head. "No, she probably wouldn't."

"So, you know the only reason she's so open to you coming into her home is because she cares about you," he said, and I nodded. "Now think about my dad. Do you really think that man would let you come into his place of business, which he guards like the three-headed dog guards the gates of Hades, if you weren't pulling your weight there?"

"No," I said chuckling. Kaden was almost as intense about his workshop as Beth was over her home.

"Now, look at me, Daniel." I looked at him. "If I didn't really care about you, if I didn't want you here, in my life, do you think I would have brought you here, would have asked you to stay?" he asked.

That one was harder. Did Joseph really care about me, or was it a pity situation?

"Joseph, I know how *I* feel about *you*, but I admit, I don't know... not really, about us... I know it isn't fair to compare you to my past, but I've trusted others who have pretended to care but ended up being hateful, even evil. Look at the situation I'm in right now. Nathan was supposed to be my closest friend, and now, every ounce of evidence points to him wanting to cause me harm, and for what? My punching him for kissing my boyfriend?"

Joseph pulled back and looked at me hard. "I can't force you to understand my feelings for you, and I can't force you to trust me, Daniel. I can only be myself and hope that eventually, you'll see me for who and what I am."

I could tell he was hurt as he let me go and walked outside. I wished I could go to him, tell him I loved him, but the situation with Nathan was raw, and I was hurting too much myself. I went to his bedroom and laid down, willing the emotional pain to stop and to give myself some time to think about how to comfort Joseph without lying about my feelings or fears.

I ended up falling asleep. I woke up to the smell of bacon, and when I walked out of the bedroom, I found Joseph at the stove, cooking. When he saw me, he said, "I figured I'd fix us breakfast for dinner tonight."

"My mom used to do that," I said and smiled at him.

"Joseph," I began. "I apologize for before, but..." Joseph turned from the stove and interrupted me.

"No, you don't need to apologize. Of course, you're struggling with trust issues right now. I can imagine what it must be like dealing with the fallout from your friend turned enemy. I'm in this for the long-term, Daniel. We're friends first, and that means a lot to me. Being your lover just makes that more difficult to accept, and I know that, so I want you to know you have all the time you need." Joseph turned the stove off, came over to where I stood and leaned over to kiss me. "Okay?" he asked.

I nodded. "Okay."

The rest of the night was much nicer. We went back up to the hot springs and soaked a while, then we came back to the cabin and made love twice.

We spent the weekend putzing around the cabin. We went for a few hikes through the woods, and Joseph showed me some of his favorite spots in the area. We even went fishing off his little harbor, and I was surprised that we brought in a nice-size coho salmon.

"Can we keep that to eat?" I asked Joseph.

"I'll have to register it with the state, but yeah, we can eat it." He smiled.

If you've never eaten fresh wild salmon, you have no idea what you're missing. Joseph took the fish and cleaned it, then went through a long process to prepare it. I eventually sat down on a reclining chair he had outside and watched him. He was steeped in knowledge about all the animals, fish, and plants in the area, and I loved listening to him slip into ranger mode as he described what we'd seen, or in this case, caught.

He was talking about how there was a growing fear that the orca, which usually survived on salmon and other fish, would eventually starve if conservation efforts weren't strictly in place. As he was talking, I dozed off.

In my dream, I was somewhere in the national park, the snowy owl perched on a nearby branch. I could tell it was concerned. I began to walk down one of the trails when I heard screaming. I could tell it was a man, but I couldn't tell where it was coming from. I began looking for the person, moving in the direction I'd heard the sound but never finding where the person was.

Exhausted, I sat down on a boulder and put my head in my hands and started to cry. When I looked up, Mr. McAllister was standing in front of me, covered in blood. He had an evil smile on his face and was carrying a large knife like a machete. When he saw me looking at him, he smiled even wider and said, "You're next."

When he lunged at me, I woke up. I was panting, and I could feel the sweat sticking to me. Joseph heard me and came over.

"What's wrong?" he asked.

I looked at Joseph in dread and said, "I think Mr. McAllister killed Nathan. I think I heard him kill Nathan!"

I figured Joseph would think I'm nuts. I didn't tell people about my dreams. Most of the time, there wasn't much to tell, but all my family had some sort of the sight. We usually laughed about how useless it was because it never really told us useful stuff like what lottery numbers would win or who would win the World Series.

Joseph looked at me concerned. He questioned me about the specifics of my dream, and I told him every part that I could remember.

"You say you think it happened in the park?" he asked.

"Yeah," I answered. After having fully woken up, I reached over to Joseph and put my hand on his arm. "It was just a dream, Joseph," I said. "I had a bad dream, that's all. All this crazy stuff about Nathan and Mr. McAllister just has me messed up in the head. Why would Mr. McAllister want to kill Nathan?"

Joseph came over and stood next to me. "Don't be so quick to toss away a warning. I've found when there are messages we're supposed to hear, the spirits tend to send them to us through our dreams. The fact that your spirit animal, the owl you told me about, was present confirms that for me."

I hadn't called the owl my animal spirit or guide or anything. I wasn't full-blooded Native American, and I knew so many people wanted to run roughshod over their cultures that I never claimed such things. My grandma had called the owl my spirit guide though, so I wasn't in a place to argue with Joseph about it.

"I'll let the guys know down at the ranger station that we need to comb the trails to see if there's any sign of your former boss or friend. I won't tell them about the dream, just that we have two missing people, one of whom was seen in town recently."

Then we both walked inside. When he got his phone, he said, "I probably should have already done that." He took his phone outside the cabin, and I could hear him as he talked to the ranger about his concern. When he came back in, he told me they were going to send out some scouts and that they'd ask the helicopter pilots, who make the rounds with tourists, to pay close attention to the trails for any possible hikers we weren't aware of.

Joseph finished prepping the salmon in the kitchen and came over to the sofa, I was now lying on and lifting my head to slide in under me. I snuggled closer to him.

"It was pretty scary to see Mr. McAllister covered in blood," I said. "Do you think it is possible that he really has killed Nathan?"

Joseph shook his head while running his fingers through my hair. "I don't know. If your dream was a warning, it could've just been telling you he's capable of murder, or it could be warning you that there was a murder. I've come to see that when a spirit sends a warning, it isn't always exactly what happened or is about to happen."

I nodded, and as I remembered the dream, I was relieved to have Joseph close to me.

When the buzzer went off on the old stove, we got up and went to the dinner table. Joseph pulled the salmon out, and while it rested, he tossed some asparagus into a hot frying pan. The salmon was possibly one of the most fantastic-tasting foods I've ever put in my mouth.

"How did you learn to cook this way?" I asked.

Joseph's smile was sad. "My mother was known to be the best cook around. She loved wild-caught salmon and had several ways of fixing it. This was my favorite, so I got her to teach me. Every time I catch salmon, I think of her," he said.

After eating, I prompted Joseph to tell me more about his mom. I could tell how much he loved her as he told one fun story about her after another.

Monday morning came too soon. Joseph was scheduled to work during the day and needed to accompany a group of scientists who had come in from Boston to see some of the wildlife in the national park. He knew he wouldn't be available much while they were there, so he asked me to leave my car. He'd drive me into town, and then Kaden would be in charge of getting me back and forth to Beth's place.

I won't pretend I didn't hate that I was being toted around like a child again, but I tried not to complain. I knew we only had one week before the court date and then, if I was lucky, we'd get everything squared away.

Of course, I couldn't have been more wrong. I stayed at Beth's until Thursday morning, helping Kaden during the day and then hanging out with Beth in the evenings. The two of them watched me like a hawk. Despite the fact I'd come to love the two of them, and they felt more like family than friends, I was ready to do myself in and save Nathan or Mr. McAllister the trouble.

On Wednesday I got a call from Joseph saying they'd found Mr. McAllister's car hidden at one of the trailheads. It had been covered in branches and debris, so people who'd driven by had missed seeing it. The Sheriff's Office had towed it into town and were doing a sweep to see what they could find.

"Well," I said to Joseph, "that means they are probably up on the mountain somewhere." Despite the warmth of the shop, I felt myself shiver. Their finding the car seemed to confirm my premonition was not just a dream, after all.

They found Nathan's body the following day. Just as in my dream, he'd been killed with a knife of some kind. Finding Nathan put the entire county and National Park Service law enforcement rangers on high alert. Helicopters were flying over the mountain in the manhunt. I was worried about Beth being alone with me. I called Joseph and told him I wasn't comfortable staying at her place, and putting her at risk. He said the Boston scientists left today because of the safety concern and that he'd be over to pick me up after he'd finished some of his duties at the park.

I called Beth and told her what our plans were and asked that she make sure to keep her house locked and alarmed until the guy was caught.

"If he is after me," I told her, "he might use you as a way to get to me. Please don't take chances, Mrs. Beth."

She agreed she would take precautions, but she was more concerned about me at the moment.

"I'll be fine at Joseph's," I told her. "We're more secluded there, and it's unlikely the guy will be able to find me."

I didn't go back to Kaden's for the rest of the week but stayed with Joseph. He kept tabs on the search and investigation, but nothing had turned up. By the time Sunday night arrived, I was ready to get back to Seattle. The police agreed to meet me at the station Monday morning, and an officer would escort me into court. We already knew that Nathan was dead, but if Mr.

McAllister knew we had court, he might be willing to come out of hiding or follow me there.

I convinced Joseph that I was fine to go on my own, which he was not at all keen on.

"Joseph, what are you going to do that I can't do on the way down there?" I asked. "You can come with me to fill my tank up, then I'll be alone in the car until I get to Seattle. If I have any trouble, I'll alert the authorities. Everyone is on the lookout for the guy, so he's more likely than not hiding somewhere up in the mountains. Besides, as far as we know, he doesn't have a car, and if he does find one, he won't know where I'm coming from. I really think we're fine with me going down alone."

Joseph was upset, but he'd been called in to the ranger station to help man a few of the different trails. Until the manhunt was over, the rangers were asked to patrol in twos. With the cuts to the Park Service, they really didn't have enough rangers for him not to be there, or at least somewhere in the park, so he'd begrudgingly agreed.

The drive down to Seattle was uneventful, as I'd guessed it would be. I phoned the Officer Sparks who'd gotten himself assigned to me as I was getting ready to turn into the station, and he met me outside the building. My court case was scheduled for eleven in the morning, and it was already ten-fifteen, so I asked him if he could follow me to the courthouse.

There were no suspicious cars following me, and when I got to the courthouse, Todd, Paul and Jeff were waiting for me at the door to the courtroom. Paul grabbed me into a hug, which still felt strange to me, but I knew he was concerned about the whole Nathan thing.

Officer Sparks escorted us all into the courtroom, and when the judge came in, Todd told him what had happened to Nathan. The judge was alarmed by the news. "You say he was killed up where you were staying?"

"I was staying outside the national park, and he was killed somewhere in the park. The County Sheriff's Office has a suspect, but they're still doing a manhunt to find him."

The judge nodded. "Son, I'm not sure you should've come in today. It might have been better for you to have your attorney call in and request a dismissal, considering the circumstances."

"Yes, Your Honor," I said. "But we were hoping by coming here today, it might flush out the suspect."

The judge dismissed the case and wished me luck.

There was no sign of Mr. McAllister, so I decided to spend the night with my brother and Jeff instead of trying to go all the way back to Port Angeles. Even though the court outcome was predictable, I was exhausted from all the drama around it. I felt horrible about Nathan, and when I closed my eyes, all I could see was Mr. McAllister covered in blood... Nathan's blood.

Yeah, he'd been a horrible friend, but he didn't deserve to die like that. No one deserved to die like that.

Jeff and Paul followed me back to the house and forced me to park my junker in the garage. "That's safer," they said. We ate dinner with little discussion, all of us thinking about the events of the past few days.

Paul asked questions about the folks in Port Angeles while we poked at the pizza we'd ordered. Finally, I told the guys that I just wanted to turn in. So, I went to bed early and texted Joseph.

Hey honey, the day went well. I'm getting ready for bed. I can't wait to see you tomorrow.

Joseph texted back immediately.

Sleep well.

Thirteen

I DECIDED TO GET an early start back the next day, and hugged Paul and Jeff goodbye as I headed for Port Angeles. I'd picked a service station that was always insanely busy to refuel, and as I guessed, nothing happened.

The three hours it took to get to Joseph's place from Seattle was never fun but being exhausted from tossing and turning the night before made it excruciating. I stopped by Kaden's to tell him I was back in town and that I was headed to Joseph's place.

He nodded and asked me to call him when I got there. I agreed and left. I texted Joseph to let him know I was on my way but didn't get a reply back. *He must be up on one of the trails*, I thought. Coverage could be bad up there.

When I got to his driveway, the hairs on the back of my neck immediately stood on end. Something wasn't right. I could feel it, sense it somehow. I pulled the car into the driveway and parked it away from the cabin, waiting to see if Joseph came out. He didn't. Again, he could've been at the ranger station.

So, I called his phone. No answer. I then dialed the station and asked if he was there.

"No, we haven't seen him all day," they told me.

"I'm at his cabin," I told them. "You might need to send someone over just in case. Something feels off."

They told me to wait for them, and I agreed. When I hung up the phone, I saw the gun and the man carrying it in the side-view mirror. I thought about punching the gas, but unfortunately, I wasn't parked in a place where I could get away. The window shattered seconds later as Mr. McAllister rammed the edge of the pistol into the glass.

"Get the fuck out of the car!" he demanded. I looked for a weapon, but before I could do anything, he said, "Try anything, and your boyfriend dies."

"What have you done?" I asked.

The sour man chuckled, and I remembered that was the sound he made when I saw him in my dream.

"*You're next,*" I remembered him saying.

The next thing I knew, he'd reached in and grabbed me by the hair. I struggled with the door, opening it so he couldn't pull me out the window. I needed to be in as good of shape as possible if I was going to survive this.

Once out of the car, he pushed me toward the cabin. "Open the door," he demanded.

What I saw when I went in would be burned on my memory forever. There was a lot of blood. Joseph was lying propped up against the wall directly across from the door. I couldn't tell if he was still alive or not. I ran toward him, but before I could get there, something smashed against my head.

When I came to, I could see the deranged man standing above me. I looked to my right and saw Joseph, still breathing, thank God. I had to figure something out before it was too late for both of us.

I started talking to divert attention away from Joseph. I knew the rangers were on their way, fifteen minutes tops. If I could distract the son of a bitch, I could at least save Joseph. Sweet Joseph. I would gladly give my life for his.

"Why are you doing this?" I asked.

"You fucking snake," he said. "You were all Nathan could think about. He was obsessed with you. I came all the way out here with him to scare you. It was his idea. He wanted you to hurt for leaving him. I thought maybe after he had time to learn what kind of sorry-ass you were, that he'd give up and see that I was what he needed. But no, you had to shack up with the local scum. He was racked with jealousy. The night I ran you over, he threw a fit and jerked the wheel back. Otherwise, I'd have been rid of you. I realized after that, he would never get over you, so we went up into the hills. One night, as he was raging about you and kept talking and talking, I got up with my knife and slit his goddamned throat."

I was speechless, but he continued to talk. "I had no idea it would feel so good to shut his mouth up. I have never hated anyone like I hate you, Daniel Porter. If it wasn't for you, Nathan would be mine and we'd be in love. You are poison. You are a snake that nips someone, and their lives are destroyed forever."

I wanted him to keep talking, hoping he wouldn't notice the rangers when they showed up.

"Now, I'm going to take from you what you took from me." He pointed the gun at Joseph. I didn't think, I just reacted. I sprang up and landed on him. The gun went off, but I could tell it missed its mark.

In a crazy rage my fists and knees made hit after hit, but the older man was stronger than he looked. Finally, he threw me off. I landed next to the front door, still desperate to keep him away from Joseph.

I lunged for the door to outside.

"You're a weak, stupid piece of shit!" I yelled. "Nathan never wanted you. He wanted to get away from you. You're old and smelly. You killed him because he never wanted you, he only wanted me. Now you're alone."

The creep came out of the house, and I ran toward the water. *Keep him away from Joseph.* That was all I could think. *Keep him away from Joseph.*

When I got to the water's edge, I turned around. He was about a hundred feet away from me. He pointed the gun at my heart, but just as I thought he was going to fire, a red burst shot out from his chest along with the point of Joseph's harpoon. The harpoon that had been hanging over his fireplace.

Mr. McAllister looked down, and seeing the harpoon, raised his gun back up. It fired just as he fell forward. The bullet hit me in the shoulder, knocking me backward.

Time slowed, and I saw Joseph appear as McAllister fell forward and I fell back into the water. I had no strength left in me, Joseph was alive and that was all that mattered.

The water rushed in over my head. I felt myself sinking, unable to move, unable to save myself.

My heavy clothing dragged me down deeper into the water. Death was slipping its arms around me. I wouldn't be able to get back to the surface to breathe. I would die in the water.

Just as I was about to give up and breathe in the water that would be my death, a dark figure passed over me. A shark, I assumed, they can smell blood. It didn't matter, death was circling me, be it a shark or drowning. Joseph was safe. I wasn't afraid of dying.

The black figure must have come around, and before I knew it, I was rising back to the surface. It felt as if I was being pushed through the water, but I couldn't tell by what. I must have fallen in and out of consciousness because the next thing I remembered was waking up in the hospital. Jeff was sitting on one side of me and Paul on the other. I immediately jumped, which caused my shoulder to ache. "Where's Joseph?" I asked, alarmed.

"He's fine. He's still being seen by the doctor."

"How bad was he hurt?" I asked.

"We don't know," Paul said. "But he came in with the other rangers and deputies when they brought you here, so he can't be too bad off. I'm sure Beth or Kaden will let us know as soon as they do."

"I've never been so afraid of anything in my life," Paul said. "When they told me you'd been shot, I thought I'd lost you."

I put my good arm, which ironically was the one I broke only a couple months before, around Paul, and Jeff came over and embraced us both. We remained like that until we heard someone clear their throat.

When we looked over, it was Joseph. He was standing in the doorway. His face was pale, and he'd been wrapped in bandages, but he was there. When I saw him, I started to cry. Joseph came over and put his head on mine.

"I'm here, my love. I'm here," he said.

"I was so afraid I'd lost you," I said. "I thought he'd killed you and I couldn't save you."

The sobs came rapidly now. The relief at seeing Joseph standing was all it took for my defenses to give in to the fear and sorrow I'd felt over the past few hours.

Joseph kept his head on mine, and when my sobs subsided, he replied, "I thought the same when I saw you go into the water. I couldn't get to you in time, and then you were just gone."

"Wh... what saved me?" I asked.

Joseph shook his head and in a quiet voice said, "It was an orca."

I'd already thought that was it, but it seemed so unrealistic, so magical... I immediately remembered the dream of the snowy owl and the orca. I figured maybe that was another prophetic dream, but I couldn't quite wrap my mind around it. Instead of trying, I said, "We are both going to be okay now, thank God. We are both going to be okay now."

Finally, Jeff pulled a chair over for Joseph, and he sat in it keeping his hand on mine. I looked over at Joseph and said, "I saw him die. I saw the harpoon go through his chest and I saw him die." Joseph just nodded, looking down. "If it wasn't for you, Joseph, I would have died instead. He meant to kill both of us, but he wanted to kill me the most."

Then I thought of Nathan, and the tears came again. "Poor Nathan, I didn't understand until that... that son of a bitch started talking, he must have fallen in love with me, and instead of admitting it, he tried to scare me. The old man was jealous, that's why he killed him, that's why he wanted to kill me and you," I said to Joseph.

Paul stepped over. "He was deranged, Daniel. He'd lost all sense of humanity. You aren't responsible for any of that."

"No, I know," I said, wiping the tears. "But I can't help feeling sad about Nathan even if he had lost his way." My brother nodded and we all fell silent.

Beth came into the room like a fresh breeze. She had flowers and balloons and began to spread them around the room. She avoided eye contact with Joseph and me the entire time, instead jabbering on and on with Paul and Jeff about how hospital rooms were sad places without decoration.

When she finally made eye contact with me, the tears started to flow.

"Damn, damn..." she said. "I thought I had that under control."

Jeff put his arm around her, and she burrowed her face into him. She quickly recovered though, and grabbing a tissue next to my bed she wiped her tears and blew her nose.

"Okay, enough of that," she said. "We will be celebrating from now on, you both survived, and your injuries are minimal, so there should be no more tears, just happiness." She almost broke down again, so she quickly added, "Now, I'm going to go find where Kaden went," and darted out the door.

Joseph smiled as his aunt left. "She's been bawling like a baby since she got here. Of course, she barreled her way into the ER, and all Dr. Barnes could do was shrug and point toward my room where they were covering every visible piece of flesh on me with bandages. Dad followed shortly behind her and held her while they finished putting me back together."

It was time for me to fight tears again. "I'm so sorry you got caught up in all this, Joseph..."

"Stop that," he demanded. "This is what it means when you're family." Then he leaned over and kissed me before adding, "This is what it means when you love someone. I would gladly give my life to save yours. And you did the very same for me tonight. I woke up when you fell on the floor beside me, and I was pretending to be knocked out, waiting for an opportunity to jump him. You beat me to it, though, when you leaped on him. I didn't realize he had the gun pointed toward me until I opened my eyes. Then I saw you dart outside and heard you taunting him and knew you were trying to keep him away from me. I will never forget how you put your life on the line for me, Daniel. That sacrifice is what gave me the opportunity to stop him."

"I love you too," I said, and Joseph put his head back on mine. The tears fell from both our eyes.

The gunshot wound seemed to be fine, so they sent me up to the ward to be observed overnight. When there was no sign of infection the next day, I was allowed to go back to Beth's.

I didn't know how I was going to explain to Joseph that I didn't have the nerve to return to where the drama had happened, where I had walked in and seen my love crumpled on the floor in a puddle of blood, and was eventually shot myself.

Beth clearly should've been a nurse. She took it upon herself to clean my wound twice daily and never flinched. I was so drugged after I broke my arm that I hadn't seen her like she was now. She bustled around the house, bringing me water, food, checking my temperature, and basically watching me like a hawk.

I loved her and enjoyed the attention, for the most part. I refused to stay in bed though. It hurt less to be shot than it did to fall off a mountain. The wound was sore for a very long time, but I didn't need to take ridiculous amounts of painkillers to survive. After the first few days, I was more than capable of surviving on over-the-counter medications alone.

Paul and Jeff refused to leave, so Beth stuck them in a cottage she said she didn't usually rent out because it could get so hot in the summer and cold in the winter. But the temperature had cooled off since we were at the end of August, and the brothers loved the place because it faced out over the sea and had lots of windows.

Paul had taken up space on the patio with an easel Beth had borrowed from some neighbor and brushes he kept in the back of the car. Artists, they were gaga over brushes, and Paul seldom went without his close at hand. I'd never seen him use them anywhere other than in his studio at home or at Jeff's gallery from time to time. I could see the little cottage from my room, and I looked out several times to see Paul standing at a canvas looking out over the Salish Sea.

At one point, I'd caught a glimpse of the painting when he had it turned toward my bedroom, and it was nothing like I'd ever seen him paint before. Paul's paintings were always serene. He was known throughout the Pacific Northwest as the man who painted happy or relaxed art. His work usually hung in attorney's, doctor's or therapist's offices where people needed to relax and chill out. This painting was anything but relaxing or peaceful.

There were streaks of red that streamed throughout the painting while black oozed from it like oil bubbling up from the surface of a tar pit. I turned away from the painting, disturbed. Paul seemed to capture my insides, the fear I'd felt when I thought I'd lost Joseph. Paul had painted despair. It only took a moment for me to realize that was the image Paul had when he thought I'd been lost. The thought of how much pain Paul must have endured mixed with my own fear of losing Joseph caused my legs to wobble, and I sat on the bed, unable to move for a moment.

Beth came in, and seeing my face, immediately came and sat by me. "Do you want to talk about it?" she asked.

"I... I'm not sure I can," I admitted. I looked at her and could only say, "I saw Paul's painting." She nodded, clearly, she had seen it too. One didn't have to be an art critic to see the anguish there.

"Come on downstairs. You shouldn't be alone when you're feeling this way. Martha is on her way over, and she's always good for a distraction. I nodded and agreed that I'd be down in a moment. I went to the bathroom and sloshed water on my face before taking her suggestion and going downstairs.

I went out to the cottage where Jeff and Paul were staying. Paul had turned the painting away when I approached. "There's no need to do that, Paul, I saw it from my bedroom window."

Paul looked guilty. Like he'd done something wrong. I went over and put my arm around him. "I feel the same way. When I thought I'd lost Joseph, that is exactly how I felt."

A tear formed in Paul's eye, but he brushed it away before it fell. "I need to paint, Daniel. This is how I process emotions. I'll destroy it when I'm done."

"No, please don't," I said. "If you've ever felt that way, ever been through that kind of torment, seeing it is a balm, at least after the initial shock that you captured the emotion so well wears off." Paul nodded and turned back to the canvas.

"Martha, Joseph's aunt, is coming over. I don't think you've met her yet. Just brace yourselves, she's as much of a live wire as Beth."

Paul smiled. "We'll be in after I get my brushes cleaned up."

Martha showed up with several hands full of food. "If I didn't know better, I'd swear you were a Southern woman, Martha," I joked after she brought in the third load of food.

She looked at me questioningly.

"In the South, if someone gets hurt, you bring food. If someone is sad, you bring food. If someone is upset about anything, you bring food, and most importantly, if someone dies, you bring food. That's why most of the people in the South are obese," I explained.

Martha chuckled. "Well, I know Beth has a house full of boys, and that *takes* food. Besides, I feel helpless not being there for you and Joseph when you were..." she trailed off and the emotion swam across her face. I went over and put my arms around her.

"We're okay," I assured her. "Everything is okay now."

"Yes... yes, it is. And now you won't go hungry," she said, wiping her eyes with her fingers. Beth came into the kitchen and saw all the food for the first time.

"What on earth is going on?" she asked.

"Martha is expressing her emotions with food like a Southern woman," I replied, making Martha laugh.

"No one has ever accused me of that before, and it's likely to never happen again."

"Martha is as Southern acting as a bird that whistles 'Yankee Doodle Dandy,'" Beth replied.

"Well, thank you, Martha, for the food," I said and hugged her.

Paul and Jeff came in shortly after, and I introduced them to Martha, who graciously shook each of their hands.

"I'm guessing you are Paul Porter, the artist," Martha asked him.

"Yes," Paul said shyly.

"I own three of your paintings," she said. "All of them are hanging in my office here in town. I'm hoping to add a fourth piece the next time I'm down at the Seattle gallery. I love the way your paintings make you feel like there is hope in a world where hope seems lost." Paul looked over at me, and neither of us mentioned his latest work.

Jeff took Martha's arm, and they went into the living room. Paul and I helped Beth move the trays of food into the refrigerator.

"I have no idea what got into that woman," Beth said. "She's not the bring food over kind of person, and when she does, she sure doesn't bring the entire restaurant with her."

"Fear of losing loved ones can drive you to do insane things you never imagined you'd do," Paul said, avoiding eye contact with me. Beth just nodded.

Joseph had gone home to do some work around the place, I guessed it was to clean up the blood and put the place back to rights. Just thinking of the cabin caused me to shiver uncontrollably. All that blood... anger, malice and blood. He got back to Beth's shortly after Martha had left.

"You look like you feel better," I told him when he walked in.

He smiled but it didn't quite make it to his eyes. There was sadness in Joseph. He knew the man had been evil, deranged, knew he would have killed us both, had already killed before, but it didn't take away the strain of knowing you were the cause of another's life being cut short. I didn't know how to comfort him other than reverting back to my Southern roots – food could only help.

"Martha brought enough food to feed several armies. Are you hungry?" I asked.

"Not really," Joseph said. "But I could use the company."

Paul, Jeff, and Beth joined us in the kitchen as I pulled food back out of the refrigerator, plated it and microwaved it for each of us. We all squeezed around Beth's kitchen table and the food did its job. We were all laughing again about silly things Paul was telling them I'd done as a kid. If they were smiling, I didn't mind being the butt of the joke for a change. It had only been a few short days since the incident occurred, but it seemed like it had been decades since smiles and good cheer had been part of our lives.

After we'd eaten, I was feeling tired and excused myself to head upstairs. Joseph came up behind me. I could tell the day had worn on him as much as his injuries had. It was still early when we crawled into bed.

"I can't shake off the depression," Joseph admitted. I turned and pulled him into my arms for a change.

"I don't think we're supposed to yet. We both probably have some PTSD to work through," I said, and Joseph nodded and snuggled into me.

"I know you aren't ready to go back to the cabin, but I feel drawn there. It's almost like I need to get back and reclaim what's mine before that asshole steals it away from me forever."

I nodded into his back but couldn't make any promises. "I'll try, but not right away, okay? Give me a little time."

Joseph just laid there. I could tell he was crying but I had nothing to help. We were both emotionally spent.

The next day, Joseph told me he was going to head up to the reservation for a couple days. He had a few friends there he thought could help out and he wanted to spend some time with them.

Reluctantly I agreed, trying to stamp down the panic that seemed to occur when he was out of sight for too long. I told Beth he'd be gone, and she put her arms around me and hugged tight.

"This is when he'll need that space we talked about the most. He almost lost you, he had to kill a man to save you, and now he is lost himself. He's a strong man, Daniel," she reminded me. "If you give him this, he'll come back to you stronger than ever."

"I know, and of course, I'll give him what he needs, but Mrs. Beth, it takes everything in me not to panic when he's away for too long. This is my trauma working itself out, I know."

"Just be patient with the process. When I lost my husband, I thought I was going to lose my mind, but time eventually made the nights less scary, less lonely. You will all get back on your feet, but you have to allow the healing to occur," she said with confidence, giving me enough to push back the hysteria for a little longer.

Paul, Jeff and I decided to take a few drives along the Washington coast. Jeff was a big fan of the *Twilight* novels and wanted to visit Forks, where they were set. So, we left early one morning and drove the hour to get there.

The area was fascinating. I still didn't quite understand why it rained there more than it did in other parts of the Peninsula, but I was sure if Joseph had been with us, he would've explained all the scientific reasons. I missed him and tried not to think about that. We ate at a restaurant covered with vampire memorabilia and then took a tour given by a local resident who had a vast knowledge of the Stephenie Meyer books, as well as pre-*Twilight* knowledge of the area.

He drove us over to the Quileute Reservation and the area where Daniel Pullen, a settler in the area, burned down their village in 1889. As the group sat in the tour van, the tour guide began to explain that the Quileute people believed they were descended from a wolf, and that's where Stephenie Meyer got the idea of making the natives shape-shifters who fought against vampires.

The next day, we explored around Port Angeles, Sequim, and eventually Port Townsend. We ate a quick lunch. Jeff and Paul wanted to tour the lavender farms along the way, and I was just glad to be distracted. By the time we got back to Port Angeles, Paul had agreed to come back and be one of the featured artists at Sequim's Lavender Festival next summer.

I got a text from Joseph that evening telling me it would be one more day before he was back. I missed him and was very disappointed I wasn't going to see him, but I understood.

Paul and Jeff felt sorry for me and decided to stay on an extra day, and this time persuaded Beth to come with us and we took a ferry over to Victoria, British Columbia.

Victoria was by far one of the prettiest parts of the Pacific Northwest, and Paul and Jeff had dragged me there on several occasions. But this time, walking through the beautifully manicured botanical gardens and seeing my brother light up with the color of the flowers and how Jeff seemed to radiate in Paul's happiness made my heart swell.

My brother was happy. I'd always been intimidated by Jeff, but now, things had shifted. I valued Jeff as I would anyone who brought that much happiness to a loved one. I eventually went over, leaned into Jeff and whispered, "I'm so glad Paul has you. It makes me happy to see the way he loves you."

Jeff was taken aback by my comment. He and I hadn't really ever spoken like this before. His eyes teared up and before any drops fell, he leaned back into me and said, "I'm just happy Paul has family that loves him as much as you do."

Beth saved us both from the mushy moment when she slipped in between us, an arm folding into each of ours as she let us escort her among the flowers.

I was bone-tired when we got back to Beth's, which was a blessing. Joseph's absence was beginning to cause my insecurities to grow. Maybe after all the horror, he'd decided this was too much. Maybe it was too much. Luckily, I fell asleep before I could ponder those thoughts too much.

The next morning, Joseph woke me up by resting his hand on my back. When I stirred and turned toward him, I could see there was a change. His eyes seemed to have regained some of the shine that had dimmed before he'd left.

"I would like you to come with me," he said. "Back to the cabin."

I felt the panic attack coming and fought to push it down. Joseph pulled me close.

"If you don't face it, it'll consume you, Daniel. I've asked two medicine men to meet us there. They're going to drive away any dark spirits that remain."

I couldn't breathe, the thought of returning scared me more than anything ever had. The blood, all the blood...

"I'm afraid, Joseph," I said emphatically.

"What are you afraid of?" he asked.

I thought of the blood, of seeing Joseph lying in his own blood in a heap on the floor, and looked Joseph in the eye. "Of losing you."

"That's why I need you to come with me. The cabin is our home, and we can't allow the darkness to gain a foothold there. You have been touched by the ancient ones. You have the power to cast out the darkness and keep it at bay forever, but only you can do that for yourself."

Joseph put his head to mine, and I felt the security of his presence reach into me.

"Okay," I said. "I'll go, but Joseph, I make no promises. When I get there, I may not be well. I may not be okay."

"If you aren't, I'll bring you back here," he promised.

I left a note on the kitchen island telling Beth I had gone with Joseph early in the morning and that we'd be back later in the day. I told her to call or text if she needed to reach me.

As Joseph drove us toward his cabin, the panic kept trying to take over. When we got to the driveway, I felt like I could crawl out of my skin, but Joseph put his hand in mine and squeezed.

"You are okay. Trust me, Daniel, you are okay."

I tried to slow my breathing and shut my eyes as we drove up to the cabin. When we stopped, I slowly opened them and in front of us stood two men. They appeared to be a father and son. Each of the men wore traditional ceremonial clothing. When they saw me open my eyes, they began to chant.

The air around them seemed to shimmer, and I was instantly put at ease.

"Can you come stand with us?" Joseph asked, and I nodded.

We got out of the car, and Joseph came around to hold my hand. I was shivering but as the men chanted, I began to feel my confidence return. Each of the medicine men took a pipe out of a satchel and lit it. They started blowing smoke around them.

As the men chanted and walked in circles around the cabin, I imagined the dark shadows moving across the earth. The men chanted for what seemed like hours, smoking their pipes, walking in circles, until there was no place around the cabin where they hadn't been.

The air smelled like ozone right after a rainstorm. The younger man lit a smudge and went inside the cabin, leaving the older man outside with us.

When they were done, they came over to Joseph and me. They blew smoke around me, and the chanting changed and became more intense. I closed my eyes as I felt like the top of my head was beginning to come away from my skull.

After a few moments, the two men pulled Joseph aside to talk to him before they left.

I needed to walk into the cabin without having a panic attack, and I was afraid I wouldn't be able to do it. I admitted to Joseph that I was a coward and I needed him to walk in with me. When we entered, I could still smell the smoke of the smudge stick. Someone, I assumed Joseph, had cleaned up all the blood, and there was no evidence that anything had ever happened. I looked at the fireplace and remembered lying on the sofa snuggled with Joseph. I looked into the kitchen and remembered Joseph cooking the delicious, fresh-caught salmon. When I wandered into the bedroom, I remembered making love to Joseph.

I walked back to the living room where Joseph stood waiting for me. "He's gone. The only thing that remains in this cabin is you and I."

Joseph came over and put his arms around me. "Do you think you can stay here again?"

"Yes," I nodded. "I think I'd like to stay here again. But Joseph?" He looked at me with anticipation and a small amount of dread.

"Yes?" he asked.

"We are going to do some serious remodeling!"

Joseph laughed and began teasing me. "What, you don't like my style?"

"No," I answered. "Old man cannot be your style."

"Aah, honey, it's deco chic," he continued teasing me.

"No," I responded. "It is old man, and there is no such thing as old man chic."

Joseph kissed me hard, then held me tight for several minutes before letting go. "If you want to redecorate, we will redecorate," he said as he hugged me again. "Are you glad you came?"

"Yeah, I'm glad. My fear's gone and in its place is peace and happiness. All I had to do was face my fears and... well, you know, I'm not the best at that. I'm glad you persuaded me."

"No problem, honey," he said. "You are strong, I knew you could do it."

"Ha, you knew, huh?" I asked, playfully punching him in the stomach, which caused him to groan.

"Yeah, that part isn't healed yet."

"Good, serves you right," I said and knelt down to kiss his stomach where I'd hit him. I looked up at him from where I was kneeling. "Where else does it hurt?"

He smiled a mischievous smile and pointed to his crotch. "Slut," I said, and he laughed, lifting me back up to my feet and pulling me into the bedroom.

Fourteen

Epilogue

D UDE, SIT DOWN AND leave Peter alone," I said as Bennett once again was asking Peter a hundred questions.

I met Bennett on one of the numerous outings by Kaden and me to finish the Seattle mansion project's many custom cabinets. He and I had hit it off when we were both trying to avoid being caught on camera and ran into one another.

"You don't want to be in the spotlight?" he asked.

I chuckled, "Well, I mean Kaden is the expert, and no... not really. I like my anonymity."

"Wish someone had warned me," he said, off the cuff.

"What? You're a famous star and you have the hottest boyfriend on the planet... well, next to mine of course."

After that we teased each other and found we had more in common than not.

As things on the mansion project sped up, I talked him into going out with Joseph and me on Peter's boat to get away. He'd never been sailing and when I mentioned that Joseph's friend did wildlife tours around the peninsula, he acted excited.

Les would've gone too, but according to Bennett, as the project neared its end, Les was working more and more. The fact that Bennett was pouting a little about that made me chuckle. When Joseph had to work a lot, I know I pouted a little myself.

Bennett laughed when I fussed at him to leave Peter alone. He had so many questions, and we'd been out for over an hour and I'd been hoping to spend a little more time with my new friend to get to know him better.

When he plopped down beside me, he admitted he always dreamed of sailing.

I sighed. "Okay, then go bug Peter, we can hang out later."

Bennett laughed. "No, I think he's had about all he wants of me for now, besides, you're right, we should be hanging out."

We spent the rest of the day laughing at the antics of the seals that swam around us or looking for other sea life.

Joseph would occasionally come over and point out some obscure thing in the water we would've missed if it hadn't been for his keen eye. Mostly, he let Bennett and I bond.

The thing we both had in common is we were shit at picking friends. The fact that his best friend before Les had been some mafia like character who was in league with his criminal father, and mine had led some half-deranged serial killer toward me wasn't lost on us.

I'd heard from Paul and Jeff's friend Cliff that they suspected Mr. McAllister had been one of the hit men in Bennett's dad's organization. Now that he was dead, there were more holes in the story than answers, but at least he wasn't alive to kill me any longer.

I hadn't realized that Bennett's dad had been one of the main gangsters involved. He divulged that one evening when he and Les had come out to spend the weekend at Beth's B&B to get away. That was Kaden's doing.

Beth had been all aquiver over them visiting... but once they arrived, it took about fifteen minutes for her to turn them into "just some of her boys."

A couple weeks after the sailing trip, I met Bennett over at his home and as we kicked back, his niece and nephews running around shooting one another with foam darts, I asked, "So, after you watched all that went down with your dad and his gang did you have nightmares?"

He nodded. "Yeah, still do. You?" he asked.

"Not as often, but when I do, they seem... more."

He sighed, "I think it's just part of the PTSD thing. I went to see a therapist a couple times and they gave me medication, but to be honest, I think seeing someone die in front of you is just traumatic. It's not something people get over."

He'd confided in me more about seeing his, well, you couldn't call Frank his friend, but the guy he considered to be his friend dead after his dad murdered him. He'd also confided how afraid he'd been for Les's life.

Both of our nightmares had been about losing our loved ones. We didn't talk much, just quick questions like this one, but those seemed to help more than anything else. Just someone who understood and could give some advice or insight on things.

That night I stayed at my brother's instead of trying to drive all the way back to Joseph and our cabin. I stared up at the ceiling in my old bedroom and wondered how I'd gotten to be so lucky. Not only had I found a true and lasting relationship with Joseph, but in the same short span of my life, I'd run into and formed what felt like a true friendship with Bennett. And not like the kind I'd had with Nathan or that he'd had with Frank.

This was one where we both benefited.

Life was funny, but damn, I felt more complete than I ever had.

Bentley's past holds him captive until he stumbles into love. Can he finally escape his past or will he lose his new found love?

Continue the Romantic Series with **Romantic Recon**

Available at your favorite bookseller!!

Join Blake's email list to get advance notice of new books and receive his occasional newsletter:

www.blakeallwood.com

MM Romance
By Blake Allwood

Transitions Series
Aiden Inspired
Suzie Empowered (MF Romance)
Bobby Transformed

Chance Series
Love By Chance
Another Chance With Love
Taking A Chance For Love

Romantic Series
Romantic Renovations (1)
Romantic Rescue (2)
Romantic Recon (3)

Melody Series
Melody of the Heart
Melody of the Snow

Road to Rocktoberfest Anthology
Changing His Tune - 2022

Coming Home Series (2023)
A Long Way Home
Family Home
Discovering Home
Finding Home
Bound For Home
…and many more

Novellas
Tenacious
Moon's Place

Romantic Fantasy
By Adam J. Ridley

Big Bend Series
Love's Legacy (1)
Love's Heirloom (2)
Love's Bequest (3)

The Witch Brothers Series
Emerald Earth (1)
Diamond Air (2)
Ruby Fire (3)
Sapphire Water (4)

Blake Allwood was born in west Tennessee, then moved to Kansas City MO after earning a degree in Early Childhood Education from Graceland College in Lamoni, Iowa. He met his husband Shaun in 1995 and they officially married in 2015, once gay marriage was legalized; although they still consider Valentines Day 1995 as their true "anniversary date". Twenty-two years later (2017), after fostering 12 children together, he and his husband sold their home, purchased an RV and began traveling the country with their two dogs.

Typically, Blake can be found relaxing in the RV or by the fire with his laptop and their Jack Russell Terrier, Buddy, curled up between his legs demanding attention. Denver, their Siberian Husky mix is often asleep at his feet or playing tug of war with Blake's husband.

Most of Blake's stories are inspired by the places they have visited in their ongoing travels. His first book, ***Aiden Inspired***, was released in 2019 and he has now written over 20 books. In 2023 he is releasing the ***Coming Home*** series which is comprised of ten-plus sweet contemporary romance novels that are based on a fictional town in his home state of Tennessee.

Blake also writes under the pen name of Adam J. Ridley for his urban fantasy fans looking for stories revolving around gay characters. His first series is The Witch Brothers Saga, starting with ***Emerald Earth***.

Books by LGBTQ+ authors